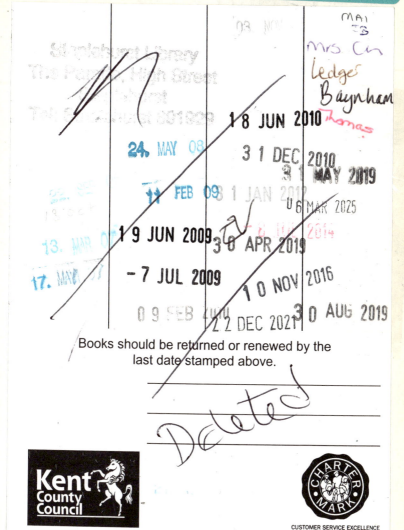

STAR ATTRACTION

To be on tour with Leon Ferrar should be a dream come true, but for Suzy Grey, his assistant, it becomes a nightmare when she finds herself in love with him. Leon is surrounded by beautiful women, from the voluptuous Toni Wells to pianist Angelina Frascana. Leon and Angelina draw close together as they prepare for a concert in Vienna, but Suzy's desperate course of action threatens to ruin her own relationship with Leon for ever.

ANGELA DRACUP

STAR ATTRACTION

Complete and Unabridged

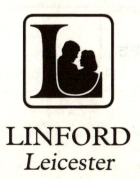

LINFORD
Leicester

First published in Great Britain in 1988 by
Robert Hale Limited
London

First Linford Edition
published 2006
by arrangement with
Robert Hale Limited
London

British Library CIP Data

Dracup, Angela
    Star attraction.—Large print ed.—
Linford romance library
1. Love stories
2. Large type books
I. Title
823.9′14 [F]

ISBN 1–84617–264–0

Published by
F. A. Thorpe (Publishing)
Anstey, Leicestershire

Set by Words & Graphics Ltd.
Anstey, Leicestershire
Printed and bound in Great Britain by
T. J. International Ltd., Padstow, Cornwall

This book is printed on acid-free paper

1

Leon Ferrar was a star. In his earlier days of self-centred youth he had been somewhat dazzled by his own brilliance. Now, however, he was beginning to recognise the pointlessness of fame and was on the whole rather weary of having to shine so brightly. But he was a true professional and knew how to keep up appearances. As far as his adoring public was concerned he was still the glamorous, hell-raising, womanising personality they had first fallen in love with.

Suzy Grey, Leon's valet, path-smoother and Girl Friday had been in his employ for six months and seven days. She had been impossibly in love with him for six months and four days, a state of affairs which she found highly unsatisfactory and somewhat humiliating. She had always imagined herself becoming enchanted with a rather serious man who would be an authority on philosophy or social history — someone like her tutors at college perhaps. Leon did not quite fit this image. What was worse he showed no sign whatever of returning her affection. She had watched the procession of vivid girl-friends who hovered on the shining periphery of his life and felt eclipsed, dull and rejected.

At the present moment Suzy was ministering to a moody and frustrated Leon in a luxury hotel in Amsterdam. He was on tour giving a series of concerts which would culminate in a final performance in Vienna, a performance which might well change the whole pattern of his career. The frustration arose from an injury to his hand which prevented him from playing the piano and driving his vintage Bentley — activities which he much enjoyed and which, in the case of the former, earned him a great deal of money. He had sliced the tendons in his thumb whilst making mayonnaise in his food processor. He was one of those men who could do everything superbly: compose and sing songs, play the piano, drive like the devil, cook like an angel — and, Suzy presumed, make love as no-one before or since. It was therefore hardly surprising that Suzy was now in that state of thwarted and desperate adoration which could produce reckless behaviour at the slightest provocation. She was keeping a very tight hold on herself. Dignity was important to Suzy.

'Hello little rabbit,' Leon said, emerging from his bedroom into the sitting-room of the fabulous penthouse suite which over-looked Amsterdam's leafy roads and shining canals.

Suzy's knees turned to slush, her mouth went dry and her heart pumped like a train. Damn! 'I wish you wouldn't call me that — I'm not in the least like a rabbit!'

He raised his eyebrows. It was unusual for her to challenge him.

He grinned with soothing, infuriating friendliness. 'No, quite right,' he agreed. 'You're far too stern and fierce to be a rabbit. I must try not to forget that!'

Suzy took a deep and clearly audible breath.

'You redheads,' he murmured teasingly, touching a strand of her fiery hair and laying his one free hand briefly on her shoulder.

The other hand was heavily bandaged to promote the most rapid healing possible and was supported in a sling for extra protection.

Suzy's skin tingled. She wished he would not touch her; she could not accept his touch as casually as he gave it. 'Is your hand any better?' she asked politely.

'No, the pain is still hellish — but I've got to get the fingers moving again. I'm going to do that concert in Vienna if it kills me.'

The Vienna concert was scheduled for a month ahead. It meant everything to Leon. The critics all said he was over-reaching himself. It was one thing to be the leader of the Silver Linings Quartet, acclaimed for their interpretation of modern and traditional jazz and for their highly individual renderings of the classics, quite another to attempt the Mozart Double Concerto before a serious and informed Viennese audience.

'Nothing's going to stop me, Suzy,' he continued ferociously, 'not my hand, my strung up nerves . . . nothing!' His intensity was such that Suzy shivered. This shift from the popular to the classical arena was so important to him. Suddenly he turned her to face him. 'Do you think I can do it?' he asked softly, staring down at her. 'Do you really think I can?'

'Oh yes. Yes, yes, yes!'

'It means a lot to me what you think,' he said, with a tender shining in his tawny eyes that turned knives in her heart. 'You're a girl of judgement, not just a pretty face!'

Suzy could hardly bear it. A girl of

judgement indeed. It was well known that Leon's preference was for beautiful blondes who dressed to be noticed, not diminutive carrot tops to be loved for their brains.

'Anything fresh on the job applications?' he asked.

She shook her head miserably. When Leon took her on it had been agreed that the job was only temporary whilst she tried to find a teaching post. She was fully trained and qualified but sadly only one of the many hopefuls chasing a very few jobs. She was not sure which prospect made her more wretched, not having the opportunity to use her skills or being offered a job and having to leave Leon.

She frequently wished that she had never met him, that the opportunity to work for him had not presented itself on a plate through the kind assistance of Bruno Saxby, a former college friend. Bruno had also trained as a teacher but more than anything he wanted to spend his life writing songs.

Leon Ferrar had used one or two of his melody lines and lyrics and adapted them for Silver Linings. Then Bruno came up with a song which Leon said looked rather promising, something that could make him a considerable amount of money. Bruno had told her about it one night, his face glowing with excitement. 'He says it needs complete revision. He's offered to let me spend a month in his villa in Austria so I can get some peace and quiet to get it done. All expenses paid. Apparently he's well known for encouraging new young talent! Phew, can you beat it?'

'No,' Suzy had said, laughing. 'Would he like to take me on as well?' She had been partly serious — and just a little desperate. Her father had recently had a second heart attack and lost his job and her younger brother Graham had got himself into the kind of scrape that ill fathers shouldn't have to be bothered with and elder sisters might just put right — if they had the cash. But Suzy, at that point, had had no immediate prospects of any employment at all.

'I'll ask him,' Bruno had declared enthusiastically. 'He was talking about needing a minder — someone to protect him from all the adoring women!'

'Thanks! Doesn't sound much in my line!' Suzy had dismissed the idea entirely.

But the next day Bruno had turned up with an invitation from Leon Ferrar to go for an interview. Within a week she was in work, with a generous wage and free board and lodging. Within two months she had been to the Continent several times, got to know the insides of a few recording studios and become sickeningly familiar with the fawning adulation of a million screaming girls as they salivated at the sight of Leon brooding over the piano under a score of spotlights.

Good old Bruno. He was a pal and she was very grateful to him. They had been friends all through college; but no more than friends — Suzy found his big pink blondness about as sexy as a hot water bottle with a furry cover. Not like Leon with his lean frame, his softly curling black hair, his powerful presence — *that* was another matter entirely.

'You'll just have to put up with me for a while longer,' Leon said, breaking into her thoughts. 'Anyway I'm so incapacitated I can't do without you. I'm going to have to cancel Bonn and Innsbruck. There's no chance of being fit enough to play by then.'

'Oh dear.'

'If I can only be fit for Vienna.' He got up and paced around the room, flexing the damaged thumb and grimacing with pain.

'You'll be O.K., Suzy. Don't worry. Once those grey-faced headmasters get a look at you, you'll be taken on right away!'

'Yes.' She felt herself moaning inwardly.

Leon was reaching inside the small refrigerator discreetly concealed amongst the shelving stacks which roamed over most of the available wall space. He took out some wine and poured two glasses. 'Come and join me in a drink,' he told her, settling himself on the huge sofa.

She sat beside him and they sipped in thoughtful silence.

'You know Suzy, you're rather special,' Leon remarked unexpectedly, his voice low and gentle.

Suzy was troubled. He had never said anything like that before. She could not believe that he was serious. She struggled to remain detached, smiling at him and shaking her head dismissively.

He was watching her; silently, languidly scrutinising until she felt a lapping of warmth in her neck and cheeks. He looked around at the opulent yet clinical hotel room with its gaudy trappings. 'You're not in the least impressed by all this are you? You don't really like it at all?'

She considered his statement carefully. 'No, I don't suppose I do,' she agreed, realising that he had judged her views about it perfectly. How perceptive he was. She longed to be able to discuss things with him, to seek his opinion and talk over ideas. She sensed that his judgements would be informed and original, guessed that his mind was both alert and expanded.

She turned her eyes towards him and her heart gave a painful leap. He was so wonderfully attractive with his chiselled features and his dark hair falling over his forehead as he sat relaxed and smiling, turning the wineglass slowly in his hand so that it glinted with little arrows of light.

He turned to meet her gaze. The smile faltered. She could hear his breathing in the silence. His face was motionless. As they stared at each other she was acutely aware of being on the brink of something immensely powerful, something unknown and dangerous.

His face was near hers. There was the smell of his skin in her nostrils making her warm and dizzy. She wished and wished that she did not want him so much.

'Suzy,' he murmured, 'Suzy.' His free arm reached out for her.

She started to form the word *no* in her throat but his lips were already joined to hers. He had wriggled out of the sling and totally enclosed her with his lithe strong arms. His fingers pressed into her back rubbing their way with insistent authority down the firm straight line of vertebrae. She began to experience a sensation of melting as though she would merge and flow into him and they would become one being.

She heard the peal of the phone as though it were coming through a distant mist. It went on pealing. On and on.

He groaned. 'Oh hell no.' As his arms withdrew she looked up at him in desperate appeal. The desire to beg and plead for him to smash the phone against the wall, lock the door and make love to her for the rest of the afternoon was so strong that it almost surfaced to her vocal chords.

But self-control won. She sat up with supreme dignity. 'I'll answer it.' That was her job after all.

The voice on the other end was calm and polite. 'We have Mr Ferrar's mail here and also a parcel to be signed and a message from the airport. It is all at the reception desk. Shall we send it up?'

'No, I'll come down now,' she said, desperate to get back on a straight and sensible course again.

'There's some mail for you,' she said briskly to Leon. 'I'll go and get it.'

He had moved across to the window. 'Yes,' he nodded. His face was turned away. She could not tell how he had been affected by the last few moments, whether his feelings were as turbulent as hers. She could feel a distance opening up again between them, stretching and expanding by the second.

She flew out of the suite and into the hush of the gleaming steel lift which sailed down to the ground floor like a swooping silent bird.

The man at the reception desk looked at her with quiet interest. She was aware of her flushed and dishevelled appearance. She hoped that no rapture showed in her face, although she felt fairly safe on that score. It had evaporated so swiftly, dwindled away into a small tight knob of miserable humiliation. The man smiled at her kindly. He handed her a parcel and two letters and pushed a receipt of delivery across the desk for her to sign.

Pausing in front of the door to the suite she tried to adjust her mental attitude in the same way that she had smoothed her ruffled hair and clothes. On no account must she allow herself to be seduced by Leon Ferrar's undoubted charm and attractiveness ever again. She meant nothing to him. She had simply been an available girl to kiss in the absence of better things.

She handed him the things and spoke with cool and impeccable politeness, 'Here you are, Leon.' She was amazed at the steadiness of her voice.

He glanced at the envelopes. One of them was addressed in turquoise ink in huge letters which roamed crazily over the entire surface. He ripped it open savagely and swore softly, as he read the note inside. He glanced at his watch, 'I've got to go out for an hour or two.'

'Shall I take you in the car?' she asked.

He stared down at her, conflicting emotions of doubt, regret and fury chasing over his strong features. The letter had clearly upset him badly. 'No. No I don't think so. Just please yourself for a while. Order dinner for seven-thirty will you?'

She nodded, wondering what was wrong.

He examined the parcel with a look of wistfulness. 'This will be the first pressing of the album for young listeners. But there's no time to listen.' He shrugged. 'You open it, Suzy. Play it and see what you think.'

Within minutes he had gone.

Suzy felt curiously abandoned. She

opened the parcel and took out the shiny new record. It had a black and silver label with Leon's name on the front. She looked at the titles of the pieces, 'Für Elise', 'Pleading Child', the Brahms Lullaby. She knew them well having struggled briefly with the piano in childhood. She placed the record on the turntable housed in the wall shelves. Her finger paused on the operating switch. She could not bear to listen to Leon and his quartet — not alone, not without his nearness. She wanted to listen whilst pressed up against him, her thighs touching his, her head laid against his chest feeling his heartbeats . . .

She went and took a shower, washed her hair and tried to feel like a new woman. Then she went out for a walk into the clamour of the city. Fresh air and exercise brought back sanity. Damn Leon Ferrar and his wretched sex appeal she thought, determined to shake herself free of his enchantment. She spent a few fascinating hours browsing in the market stalls, bought some postcards and wrote to her family as she sat drinking hot chocolate in one of the street cafes.

She arrived back at the hotel in much improved spirits.

The man at the reception desk greeted her politely.

'Is Mr Ferrar back?' she asked.

The man glanced through the heavy swing glass doors. 'I think he is arriving just now.'

She turned. She saw Leon getting out of a taxi, his face dark and turbulent with concealed irritation. One arm was wedged firmly in his sling, the other held out stiffly to the occupant of the taxi.

Suzy stared in open fascination as a beautiful blonde woman stepped out, almost falling over as a result of the tightness of her skirt and the skyscraper tallness of her heels. She smiled engagingly at the small cluster of handsome young porters who seemed to have materialised from nowhere and gestured helplessly to the boot of the taxi whose lid was springing open over a tightly wedged cargo of cases and bags.

The porters started to unload. The woman watched anxiously. Leon stood looking quietly murderous on the pavement then sprang up the steps and disappeared into the lift without so much as glancing to left or right.

His blonde companion made astoundingly slow progress into the hotel. She kept pausing — adjusting her hemline, her neckline, her hair, her glittering gold ear-rings. It was as though she expected flash bulbs to be popping, a little round of applause as she posed gracefully at the top of the steps before passing through the glass doors and erupting into the foyer. She might have been disappointed at the lack of a full Press reception but there was no lack of male attention and appreciation. Every single man in the foyer looked — and looked again for she really was a stunningly beautiful girl — soft curly blonde hair, bluebell-mauve eyes, a slim but curvy figure and long shapely legs. She was gloriously tanned in a glistening unmistakably Californian style and her skin from head to toe was firm and flawless.

She gazed around her helplessly. She looked like the sort of girl who required one man constantly at her elbow as well as the admiring eyes of many. Suzy frowned, wondering what she should do to help. Although the blonde girl's arrival had shattered her briefly recaptured composure, as though someone had squeezed all the breath out of her lungs, she nevertheless felt compassion for her. The girl looked lost and hurt, like a downy nestling bird exposed to a winter blizzard.

Suzy walked up to her and smiled. 'I'm Suzy Grey,' she said with friendly firmness, 'Mr Ferrar's assistant — temporary assistant,' she added hastily.

'Oh my God!' The blonde gaped at her uncomprehendingly.

'I don't get it! You mean you're here

all the time — with Leon?'

'Yes.'

'Oh my God!'

'It's quite all right,' Suzy said coolly — 'I shan't get in the way.'

'Oh' — the girl looked at her with fresh interest. After a few seconds she smiled with unmistakable relief. 'Suzy,' she said warmly — 'I didn't mean to be rude. We'll get along just fine.' She wriggled her shoulders about and giggled seductively. 'I'm Toni,' she said, 'Toni Wells?' She looked at Suzy expectantly.

Suzy, well aware that Toni had sized her up and dismissed her as being no competition whatsoever for Leon's attention, also realised that Toni was asking for the flattery of recognition. 'Oh yes — I've heard of you!' she reassured her, recalling the odd photograph in newspapers and Graham's remarks on Toni's bust size.

'Say — you're nice. We'll get on just fine,' Toni repeated.

'Where am I supposed to be going?'

'Penthouse Suite.' Suzy told her crisply.

Toni vanished into the lift along with a crush of cases and a porter. She left behind a lingering cloud of heady perfume. The man at the desk smiled at Suzy in what looked like sympathy. She smiled back trying to look dispassionate. Deciding that it would be tactful to allow an interlude of a few minutes to elapse before returning to the suite, she walked up and down the glass display cases flanking the foyer. The diamond jewellery, the cut crystal and the hand-painted china were of no more than passing interest.

She was soon wondering what to do next.

Then, with a thrill of shock, she noticed a silent lady with deeply hooded eyelids standing beside the bar, vigilant and immobile, a sophisticated camera slung around her neck. Her shiny black-button eyes were fastened on Suzy and the opalescent orb of the camera glinted hopefully in anticipation of a task to be undertaken. Suzy recognised her as one of the journalists who pursued Leon with grim doggedness, ever hopeful of some juicy titbit to send to their newspaper. Did the woman have a licence to follow him around, Suzy wondered. It shouldn't be allowed. Presumably there was nothing to stop her. She knew that Leon was accustomed to handling the darker aspects of his fame. But how wearying it must be for him.

The man at the desk was calling her, jolting her out of her thoughts. 'Miss Grey,' he was saying courteously.

She turned to him with a questioning smile.

'May I order you something while you wait?' he asked. 'Coffee — a beer perhaps, some wine?'

His impeccable yet friendly consideration warmed her.

Why not, she thought, looking at the shiny glass tables and the fat squashy chairs where laughing groups of guests sat relaxing over drinks.

'We have very good local beer,' he went on, 'very cool from the cellars.'

'A beer would be lovely.' She went to sit down feeling pleasantly cherished. A waiter arrived almost immediately with a glass of pale frothing beer. She got out money to pay. He shook his head. The drink was obviously going to be charged up to Leon's account.

She shrugged and smiled to herself. She did not think it would matter.

A young man in jeans and open shirt flopped down next to her.

He was lean and golden with pale almost white blond hair.

'Good evening,' he said in the carefully articulated manner of people whose native language is not English.

'Hello,' Suzy said, taking an instant liking to the friendly, cheerful way in which he smiled at her.

'Are you here on holiday?' he enquired.

She started to explain and soon they fell into easy conversation.

He was a student on holiday with his

parents in Amsterdam before flying down to the South of France to join friends on a camping holiday. 'We shall be wind-surfing — all the time I hope. It is a wonderful sport.' His eyes shone with enthusiasm. He began to explain the intricacies of the sport to her, then broke off and laughed. 'I am boring you,' he said.

She shook her head. He had taken her mind off Leon and his fiercely wonderful kisses for a moment. Allowed her — just for a moment — to forget that some other woman might be sharing those kisses instead. Given her the peace of not having to quiz herself on whether she cared or not. She smiled warmly at him.

'Perhaps you would like to see a little of the city with me this evening?' he suggested. 'The nightlife is very good!'

She hesitated. She would have liked to accept the invitation but she was again uncertain as to whether she would be on duty or not. Perhaps Leon would need her.

As the young man sipped his beer and smiled at her encouragingly she noticed Leon stepping out of the lift. He searched the foyer with a wide glance which quickly located her. His eyes moved over her with sinuous, lazy appraisal as though he wanted to remind himself of every line and curve of her face and body. She felt a flame of scarlet in her cheeks and a twisting stab in her chest.

She knew that he had noticed the young man by her side, eager and attentive. He was still looking thunderous, although Suzy had no reason to believe that she was the cause. If only she were. If only he cared enough about her to be jealous that another man was showing interest. He came towards them, looking down at them with careful appraisal. He nodded politely to the Dutchman, then said to Suzy, 'I've been wondering where you were.'

Suzy had the feeling that he would really like to have asked her where the hell she had been but was too poised and controlled to do so.

An elegant formally dressed blond couple in their forties came to sit by the young man. His parents obviously. They spoke in rapid Dutch. The young man smiled apologetically at Suzy, 'I must go,' he said, 'get ready for dinner. My parents are very hungry. Perhaps I may see you later?'

'Yes . . . perhaps.'

She watched him stroll off to the lift with an easy confident stride. She looked questioningly at Leon.

'You make friends easily, Suzy,' he commented, his eyes moving from the young man to her face and then to the empty glasses on the table.

'Yes Leon, I do,' she agreed. 'With both sexes,' she added very firmly. She was not going to allow him to suggest that she was a little flirt — and somehow she did not think that he really believed that.

'So,' he drawled, 'you will be seeing the handsome young blond later perhaps. You have a liking for blonds,

Suzy?' he teased lazily.

She ignored the latter remark. 'I may be seeing him later. I haven't decided yet. And of course I was going to check with you first to see whether you needed me before I decided anything.' There was great resolve in her voice.

His lips twitched. 'You're a fierce little thing,' he said mockingly. 'I'm becoming quite scared of you!'

He leaned back in his chair and looked around the foyer, buzzing now with activity. He noted his hooded eyed pursuer, her hand with its long red nails clasping the camera like a lobster's claw. His face remained blank and emotionless. He relaxed his lean frame and allowed his eyelids to droop for a fraction of a second. Suzy's quick eye took in the lines of fatigue around his mouth, the depth of weariness in his tawny eyes, softly dark in the shady foyer. Something curled into a tight knot in her heart. Of course he needed her. She would write the young man a little explanatory note and leave it with his parents. There would be other nights for her to go out. She got up.

'Don't go!' he said sharply. 'Stay and talk to me.'

'I'm going to order you a drink,' she said softly. 'You look as though you need one.'

His eyes closed again and a slight shudder moved over his features. When he opened his eyes again the glance was like midnight velvet, tender yet darkly provocative. 'Aah, how wonderful to be looked after,' he drawled, 'and by a beautiful red-head too.' His tone was playful and teasing. It hurt her, made her feel as though he was ranking her in his string of fillies. The little chestnut no doubt! It was really too bad of him. She must stop thinking there was some special rapport between them.

She ordered him some chilled white wine and perched dutifully on the end of her chair to talk to him as he had requested.

'You met Toni — I gather?' he added.

'Yes.'

'She's getting ready for dinner,' Leon commented drily. 'Has been for the last half hour. She should be ready in another three quarters.'

Suzy wondered what Toni had been doing before that? Making love with Leon possibly. Was that why he looked so tired? She smiled politely.

'Isn't it time you got ready, Suzy?' he asked looking pointedly at her casual attire.

'Yes,' she said slowly, 'I suppose so.'

'I want you to dine with us, Suzy.'

'Oh no! I couldn't.'

'All right then. I'm not asking you. I'm telling you. It's part of the job. Probably worth treble rates.'

'But Leon — Toni will be . . . '

'I want you to be ready in half an hour. O.K?'

Suzy sighed. Leon was used to people doing as he asked, she supposed.

She went to her room and changed into a soft cotton jersey dress in dark navy. She tied a soft bronze belt around her waist and put on matching bronze pumps. She could hear Toni through the wall splashing energetically in the bath. She was singing in an attractive although not especially tuneful voice. Suzy wondered how she would look in full dinner regalia. Pretty spectacular, she judged.

Suzy was not displeased with her own appearance as she looked in the mirror. The sun had teased out a host of butter-scotch coloured freckles and brought a fresh beaming rosiness to the skin on her face, neck and arms. It was as though she had been given a present — something to make her look just that little bit special and different. The turbulence of the last few days made her suddenly bold and filled her with an attitude of 'who cares' and 'so what'! She put on some bright coral lipstick and let her hair free so that it swung in amber brilliance around her face. She sprayed herself with the exotic 'Jungle Gardenia' which a friend had brought over from the States and felt prepared

— perhaps not for anything — but for most things.

Returning to the foyer she was disappointed not to see Leon. The waiter brought her a menu and another chilled beer. The choice of food was delicious but exclusively French *haute cuisine*. Suzy hoped that she would have the chance of sampling some of the simpler local fare on another occasion.

After a few minutes had gone by she became aware of a slight but unmistakable hush trembling over the foyer. A dramatically striking couple were emerging from the lift. The man tall, strong, languid and yet powerfully attractive — the woman blonde, curvaceous, dizzily pretty and outrageously sexy. Toni's dress was an emerald and silver slither of glistening tubular beads which glided softly over her curves. The hem was cut in graceful scallops and the skirt slit to the thigh on one side. The dipping neckline revealed a good deal of her beautifully rounded breasts and the butterfly-shaped flash of diamond and emerald stones nestling amongst her blonde curls completed the breath-taking effect to perfection. She clung to Leon with fervent possessiveness and gazed up at him adoringly.

Suzy rose to greet them, feeling like a wren in confrontation with a brightly plumed canary.

'You look lovely, Toni,' she said quietly. She did not look at Leon — did not trust herself to remain calm.

'Hey, Suzy — have you eaten yet?' Toni said. 'What do you think I should have?'

'She's eating with us,' Leon cut in coolly.

Toni dropped her arm and glared at him in horror.

He tightened his lips viciously. 'I hope you're not in the mood for making a scene?' he told her icily.

Toni pouted. Suzy saw the signs of tears welling up, the sudden reddening and swelling around Toni's eyelids.

'I'm sorry, Toni,' she said, 'I won't get in the way.'

She could have murdered Leon for treating them both so badly, humiliating Toni, embarrassing her. Yet she felt there was no alternative to going along with his plan. It must be an artist's whim. She would try to forgive him.

They sat round the table in a joyless triangle. Toni sulked openly. Leon was withdrawn and impassive and Suzy tight with indignation. They progressed through lobster bisque, pâté en croûte and on to the petit poussin and mange-touts. Toni ate hardly anything. She must be very upset Suzy thought sympathetically; herself extremely hungry and having thoroughly enjoyed the food if nothing else.

'It's a shame to starve, Toni — ' Leon remarked — 'when there's so much good food available.'

'I can't eat all this high cholesterol junk,' Toni complained. 'I have to watch my figure. You know that!'

'No, no,' Leon chided softly, 'I'll watch it for you.'

Toni gazed at him, uncertain of how to interpret this remark. Suddenly she broke into a big smile. 'Oh, you're so gorgeous!' she cooed. 'I could just love you to pieces!'

A muscle twitched in Leon's temple. 'Try to restrain yourself, Toni. We British are a very dignified race.'

Toni giggled, ordered prawns and coleslaw vinaigrette and began to look happy again.

Suzy tried to absorb herself in the serious business of choosing between hazelnut gâteau or fresh peaches in brandy. She decided on the peaches. They were exquisite — afloat on a drunken sea of golden syrup. She ate them very slowly, delighting in each mouthful. She glanced up and was instantly locked into a piercing gaze from Leon.

He was watching her — a heavy sultry expression in his eyes — as though he would devour her very slowly, savour her as she had just savoured those plump exotic peaches.

A ferocious bright spark of anger kindled in Suzy's head. The man was impossible. He must be insatiable needing two women to toy with at the same time. He was like some enchanting, irresistible Arab prince — but she had no wish to be one of the harem.

With decisiveness rather than dignity she got up from the table, crumpled her linen serviette into a ball and prepared to leave the dining-room. 'I'm sure you will not be needing me any more this evening,' she told Leon, flashing him a look of glinting steel which would have had most men trembling. 'I would like some time to myself!'

'Say Leon, Suzy could use some time on her own,' Toni agreed, all smiles now. 'The night is young,' she said seductively.

'Granted,' Leon said quietly. His look was lazily detached, his eyes now blank and veiled yet Suzy felt that she had seen some fleeting tender reproach in them, that she might just be deserting him — perhaps even wounding him.

But that was ridiculous. She must stop going soft on him; he was a hard man. He needed treating as such.

She stood in the lift feeling stormy and conflicted. She thought of the tall young Dutchman. Was it too late to go and find him, take him up on his invitation?

Impulsively she clamped her fist on the stop button and re-programmed the lift to descend again. She could not see the young man in the foyer. It was anybody's guess where he was now. So much for her delicate consideration of Leon and his needs. He had completely ruined her evening.

Sitting quietly in her room she heard Leon and Toni return to the big reception room next door. There was a hum of voices, Toni's tinkling laughter and an echoing tinkle of glasses. A wave of heat swept through Suzy's body like moving sunlight over a hillside. She could not bear to sit on her own next to Leon and one of his ladies for one more second. She gathered up shoulder bag, a light knitted jacket and her courage and decided that a quick look at Amsterdam at night would do her a lot of good.

Walking past Leon's door it occurred to her that it would be polite to let him know that she would be out for a while. She could still hear voices, SO it seemed safe to give an enquiring knock.

'Come in.' His voice was calm and relaxed.

Suzy was confronted by the disconcerting sight of Toni sitting on Leon's knee, her upper body twined around him like a passionate python. She was nibbling and licking at his left ear and crooning to him in the wheedling fondling fashion Suzy had noticed her using with him earlier.

Suzy felt a little shocked as though she had burst in on her headmistress wearing underclothes. 'Oh I'm sorry!'

'No need,' Leon pushed Toni gently away and slid her onto the sofa as he got up and came to stand by Suzy in the corridor, closing the door behind him.

'What can I do for you?' he asked raising one eyebrow in casual appraisal. He seemed totally unconcerned by the situation — even slightly amused.

Suzy's anger burst out of the tight chains in which she had enclosed it for the last few hours. 'You can stop humiliating me and your girl-friend in there!' she said in a soft icy hiss of fury.

'Really!' Leon slid a wicked glance at her. She felt that he was laughing silently.

Her fury intensified. 'When I took on this job I had no idea that it involved playing the biggest gooseberry of all time. And I have no intention of doing so. Think how that poor girl must feel!'

Leon smiled with infuriating sympathy — 'Ah!' he mused, 'and how did you feel, my little vixen?'

Suzy's eyes snapped with astonishment. 'Don't!' she cried, 'I'm not a machine for you to switch on and off when it suits you. I've come here to do a job. Just let me get on with it and don't involve me in your love affairs. I absolutely refuse to be used in that way.' Her resolve was solid as rock.

'Are you resigning, my little fireball?' he queried gently, twisting one of her fire-bright curls around a slender finger.

'I'm not your little anything,' she hissed in fury.

She jerked her head. The curl tightened on his finger but she wrenched it free, wincing with the sharp pain. She turned her face to him. His look was unaccountably tender again, but she did not, could not believe in him. Underneath that kind look she knew that he was uncaring, callous, cruel even.

The thought of losing the job shocked her out of her anger. Instantly she was subdued with the possible misery of not seeing the mission through, not being able to bail Graham out of his silly adolescent scrapes. Something else struck her like clamps of iron closing around her heart.

'I'm a prisoner,' she whispered to

him, 'a prisoner here with you because I need the money — I haven't even the funds to get home!'

He tilted his head to one side and considered. 'Mmm — yes! That is a somewhat dramatic way of stating things — but perhaps quite apt.'

He paused, laid a hand gently on her shoulder as she stood there her head drooped in dejection, 'Suzy — it'll all be fine soon. It's just a difficult time at present. Trust me?' His voice was low and urgent. But how could she trust him. She again looked up into his face. Perhaps she could. What choice was there?

'I'm going out for an hour or so,' she said resignedly.

His brows came quickly together in a dark frown.

'Like hell you are. You don't go out in Amsterdam alone after dark.' He gripped her upper arm in a firm vice.

She stared at him. He might well have a point, but she was her own mistress after all. He had no right to interfere with her free time.

'Ah,' he said slowly, 'I remember now. You were arranging a rendezvous with the handsome Dutchman. I mustn't detain you, Suzy!'

Let Leon think what he liked, she concluded wearily. Just as long as she could have a space to think, some time on her own without the constant ache and conflict of his troubling presence. His eyes held hers with dark intensity for no more than a splintered second. Then he was gone — back to his luxurious lair . . . with the delicious, tempting Toni.

She was free! She would take no more than a brief walk to look at the city's bright lights.

So Suzy, normally so rational and level-headed, who would never have dreamed of walking alone in the dark streets of London, went out into the soft blue evening of Amsterdam, unescorted, lonely and very vulnerable as she was soon to find to her cost.

2

The pavements were still warm as though they had stored up the sunshine of the day for the benefit of night-time pedestrians.

Little bars and discos were filled with pools of yellow and peach-coloured light and the sound of music and laughing voices leaked from their doors out into the streets. Suzy could smell wonderful savoury smells — sausages, onions, vinegar and garlic dressing. There were shops, brilliantly illuminated displaying beautiful clothes in vibrant colours, sleek modern furniture, electronic equipment and precision watches. Everything was arranged in a subtly but unmistakably different way from the shops in London reminding Suzy that she was in a foreign place. Dreamy delicious images of the glamour of the Continent poured through her veins giving her the enthusiasm and confidence to venture right away from the hotel and through into the theatre and entertainments quarter.

The streets here were quiet, presumably as performances were taking place and the auditoriums still filled with the crowds who would later throng the pavements. She walked along slowly, pausing occasionally to look at posters advertising plays and comedy shows. There were some explicit appetisers for strip shows in the form of lurid cartoons or glossy posters. She felt worldly and tolerant, smiled indulgently as she passed.

A well-dressed, pleasant-looking man walked up to her with purpose as she stood trying to puzzle out the writing on a poster outside a small fairy-light decked theatre door. He spoke to her very politely. She turned. She knew that he was not speaking Dutch but could not identify what language he was using. Whatever he was trying to tell her, she did not understand. She smiled her warm open smile and shrugged her shoulders.

The man came closer, put his face near hers. 'English?' he suggested.

'Yes!' She smiled with automatic relief.

'You would like a drink — yes?'

Her mind reeled. 'No, no thank you.' She turned with sharp rejection.

He placed a restraining hand on her arm. 'Please — you come for a drink. We talk — no?'

'No!'

He persisted. 'We have a nice time. I pay well.'

With sick horror Suzy noticed the notes in his hands, heard the rustle of paper currency. He was offering money for services to be rendered. She gave a whimper of dismay.

The man frowned. 'What is the matter? You walk here alone; you walk very slowly down the street. I watch you. You look for a man — yes?'

'Please,' she cried, 'go and find someone else. You've made a mistake.'

'But I do not want someone else. I want you. I like you. Very pretty.' He touched a strand of her bright hair.

'No. Please no. Go away!'

Now he was angry. His hand grasped her upper arm, the fingers bruising the tender flesh.

She shook herself free in desperation and plunged down an alley running by the side of the theatre. Blood roared and thundered in her ears. She stumbled over dustbins and empty milk bottles. A cat screeched in protest and fled into the night brushing its spiky threadbare tail against her leg. She felt sick, retched a little. Instinctively she had wrapped her arms round her breasts for protection. She glanced down the alleyway. The man had not followed — which was just as well. The alley had led to a complete dead end where plenty of unpleasant things could have happened to her without anyone being any the wiser. She did not know how long she sat in dumb terror and misery on an old dirty beer crate.

Eventually she dredged up all her courage and re-entered the main street.

She tried not to run, tried to appear calm and aloof but it was a massive effort. Her whole body was shrieking with fear. Her throat was so dry that she could hardly swallow. She thought she had returned on the same route she had set out on but the streets looked confusingly alike. The venture had started in such unplanned haste that she had forgotten her street map. She realised what a stupid, impulsive fool she had been — to open herself up to all the dangers that a vibrant city, notorious for its exciting night life could offer an unprotected, slight young woman like herself.

Leon had been quite right to be so angry and forceful in vetoing her plan. She wished she had listened to him. She hurried on. It was late now, eleven o'clock, eleven-thirty, going on for midnight. No one spoke to her, no one accosted her, yet every man she saw was an enemy — looking at her as a possible source of fun for the night, to be paid off and discarded like used merchandise in the morning.

Suddenly, with relief, she recognised a street name. But she still had a ten-to-fifteen-minute walk before reaching the hotel. She was exhausted. She ploughed on with determination. A man approached, large and bearded. He slowed down as he came nearer. Her heart leapt crazily like a caged tiger. He was talking, talking — and smiling. He had an opened-out map, but Suzy did not realise that he was simply asking for directions; her feelings of fear and total exposure were pushing all perception and reason aside.

She started to run. She ran and ran until there was the taste of blood in her throat. In front was a tall dark figure, striding ahead. He kept stopping, looking in doorways, peering down side streets. The walk was familiar — the easy stride, the long legs, and the slim hips.

'Leon!' she called fervently but her

voice was strangled and powerless. Her relief and joy were so great that she stumbled a little. Her legs were heavy like great grotesque limbs in a dream; she would never be able to reach him. 'Leon,' she shouted panic-stricken now, in case he disappeared. 'Leon! It's me, Suzy.'

He turned, stopped dead, then came running to her with long swift strides. She flew into his arms, put her hands inside his jacket to feel the warm reassurance of his body, laid her head on his chest and listened in amazement to the great choking sobs which sprang out of her throat and split the quiet darkness.

His presence was deeply reassuring but his words were harsh. 'You crazy little fool,' he said, 'What on earth do you think you've been doing? Tantalising every man in Amsterdam, going out in the streets on your own looking as edible as a bowl of strawberries. I could kill you. I've been searching the damn city looking for you for the last two hours. I saw that young Dutchman in the bar and realised that you'd gone off on your own!'

'Oh,' she moaned. 'I'm sorry to have been a nuisance.'

'A nuisance,' he growled, 'don't you ever do this to me again.' He was shaking her — hard. She did not mind. His chastisement was reviving her. Soon she would be fighting back. She felt so safe with him. He clamped a ferociously violent arm around her shoulders and set off at a furious pace dragging her along with him. 'Have you been O.K?' he asked grimly.

'No. A man propositioned me!'

'The rat! I'll murder him.'

'He didn't follow me — but I was so frightened.'

'Well let's hope that'll teach you not to be so out of your mind idiotic!'

'Yes,' she said humbly. 'I think it will.' She looked up at his fierce dark profile and was enormously grateful for his presence, for his concern. He need not have made her his responsibility like this — not to the extent of abandoning his beautiful lover to search for his wayward assistant.

He bundled her through the hotel door and almost threw her ahead of him into the small late-night bar. 'Brandies!' he told the barman.

'Drink it,' he ordered Suzy.

She gulped it down obediently. The fiery warmth spread through her body instantly.

'You look a bit rough, Suzy,' he commented in dry tones.

'Yes,' she admitted ruefully. 'I'll be O.K. soon, really!'

'I should hope so,' he said curtly. Then suddenly he smiled.

Suzy felt the world around her spring into magical life, felt a warm internal glow that had nothing to do with the brandy. Looking into his face she noticed a new bruise on his cheek bone.

'Leon — what have you done?' she asked, tentatively touching the damaged skin with a gentle finger.

He pulled away in exasperation. 'One

of life's little mishaps,' he growled softly, staring at her in steely confrontation until she dropped her eyes to her hands.

'I'm sorry — I didn't mean to intrude,' she murmured.

His jaw was tight with an angry, frustrated look like some wild animal tethered and desperate to be free.

'Forget it,' he commanded.

She was silent, finished her brandy.

With unexpected gentleness he asked, 'Are you all right now?'

'Yes.'

'Good,' he raised a sardonic eyebrow at her, 'I hope you stay that way. I want you up and ready to drive at seven-thirty tomorrow morning. Mmn — this morning,' he said pointedly looking at his watch. 'There's been a change of plan. We're going straight on to Vienna. I don't much care for the life-style here.' His eyebrows lifted again in rakish suggestion.

Suzy felt vaguely worried. 'Oh — I see.'

'Toni's going to stay at the villa for a while and you and I are going to get down to some work.'

'Does Toni know about this?' she asked — somewhat needlessly. The vivid spanking fresh bruise on Leon's face told a graphic story of the fiery scenes which must have taken place when Toni learned of the plan to remove her to Austria like some parcel.

'I'd rather not comment,' he said coolly. 'I'm sure you've guessed everything, Suzy. Your blue eyes seem to beam down into my poor weak soul in ice-hot beams of disapproval.'

'No,' she said defensively, searching for something to say that would be bland and soothing without angering him further.

He got up impatiently. 'Come on,' he ordered, 'it's time you got some rest. Bad enough having to put my life in the tender hands of a female driver, without having to worry about whether she's totally clapped out and useless from the excitement of a hectic night life!'

'I'll be just fine,' she replied in slightly heated tones. 'You'll be perfectly safe with me!'

★ ★ ★

The big car moved sedately out of Amsterdam and onto the south-bound motorway. The day was one of dazzling gold sunshine polishing the surface of the road to gleaming blackness.

Suzy concentrated on her driving carefully scanning the black snaking road ahead. Leon sat at her side, grimly surveying the map, and reading out the place-names which became realities as they progressed on, clusters of buildings which appeared briefly to the east and west of the motorway.

'No need to drive like a maniac,' he growled, noting that the speedo needle indicated that they were travelling at over one hundred miles per hour. He was a terrible passenger, clearly seething with irritation at not being behind the wheel himself. He drummed his fingers on his knee, discouraged any attempt at conversation, refused to have the radio or cassette on and was altogether as jumpy as a caged tiger. His long frame was taut with a fettered angry frustration which pervaded the interior of the car.

Suzy, her hands holding the wheel with perfect competence, was internally gripped with some anger of her own. Watching Leon at 7 a.m. that morning usher the pink-eyed Toni into a taxi to take her and her chaos of luggage to the airport, had reawakened her feelings of hostility towards him. She felt a cold fury that he should presume to treat Toni in this way; use her as a pretty toy and then dispose of her because her presence was tiresome and embarrassing. She saw it as the colossal egoism of a devastatingly attractive man who gave himself the licence to select and appropriate pretty women, as though from a display of glittering merchandise and then put them back on the shelves when it suited him. Her anger was tinged also with a deep disappointment. She had really begun to believe that he was a better person than this. But how could she go on deluding herself when she had seen the evidence with her own eyes. The high-handed contempt, the casual attitude to sex, the cold rejection; that was how he treated women. Poor Toni!

Suzy was full of sympathy for the undeniably well endowed, voluptuous blonde.

By two o'clock Suzy's eyes and head buzzed with pain and her limbs quivered with the effort of constant vigilance.

'Turn in at the next service point,' Leon told her tersely, instantly alert to her soft sigh of fatigue.

They stopped, re-fuelled the car and freshened up in the cloakrooms.

Suzy declined to eat anything, had a drink of fruit juice and a peach and was anxious to press on. Leon, making his way through a glass of local beer seemed to be shedding his unease. He smiled lazily at her but she jumped up, avoiding his eyes. The power of his smile alarmed her, told her she was still vulnerable to his charm.

'Are you tired, Suzy?' he asked.

'I'm fine,' she said in bright tones.

'Perhaps you should have a rest,' he mused, 'motorway driving is pretty wearing.'

'No, we need to get on, don't we?' She was already walking away from him towards the car-park.

She started the engine and pulled the car out once again to join the furious hurtle of traffic on the motorway. There was an accident a little further on. Police car sirens wailed and a black helicopter hovered overhead like a brooding insect.

'This damn road is like a vampire — out for blood!' He consulted the map. 'We'll take the country route,' he told her quietly, 'no need to kill ourselves. We can take an overnight stop.' They turned off the road, left its crazy clamour and found themselves in the calm green sanity of the countryside, on a quiet road which threaded its way along the base of a wide valley. There was a light licking breeze now, teasing the white furls of cloud. The hills stood out against the sky, some peaks thrown forward in clear silhouette, some reticent and blue-misted. As they drove deeper into the countryside the slopes became thickly clad with dark green forest from which the odd timber clad house poked engagingly. Stretching skyward in a solid grey mass they saw a turretted castle.

Leon pressed a button to make his window slide silently down, then grunted softly as the sweet air stroked his face. 'Ah,' he said with feeling, 'peace. Calmness. A chance to breathe.' She felt his eyes swerve towards hers. 'Just you and me, Suzy. All alone!'

Her heart lunged against her ribs, 'Yes,' she replied with careful non-committal.

'What's the matter?' he asked calmly.

She felt her nerves screech. 'Nothing,' she told him.

'Oh yes there is!'

'No.'

'Tell me, Suzy!'

'Leon — please. I'm driving!' Incredibly tears were showering in the back of her throat.

'Yes. I'd better not break your concentration. You're a good driver, Suzy.'

'Thank you.'

'Better than most,' he added with a hint of teasing.

'Than most women?' she enquired defensively.

'No — than most anybody.'

'I thought perhaps you were prejudiced against women drivers,' Suzy said with half-hearted apology.

'No, not really,' he said. 'There was a girl I knew once,' he continued, his voice soft and reflective, 'she killed herself behind the wheel — speeding, showing off a little. You know the sort of thing. It was a total waste of a promising young life.'

'Oh — how terrible,' Suzy said in genuine sympathy. 'I can understand now why you dislike speed.'

He was silent for a few moments, then he shrugged. 'Yes — well perhaps it's time I got over it. As a matter of fact I'm beginning to feel very safe with you. Perhaps you'll help me to kill the anxiety and enjoy the thrill of speed. Do you think so, Suzy?'

'I hope so — if at all possible,' she said politely.

She felt his eyes on her, watchful, enquiring. Eventually he switched on the radio and managed to locate some Brahms through the crackle and hiss of a welter of foreign stations. He drummed his slender fingers thoughtfully on his knee. From time to time he resumed his gaze of slow appraisal as she struggled furiously to combine alertness with calm composure.

By the side of the road a river glittered as it twined itself through the grass in plump loops.

'Stop here Suzy,' he commanded gently.

She was startled.

'Just here,' he said reassuringly. 'You can pull over on to the grass. Switch the engine off, will you.'

She stared stubbornly at the dappled, glistening water, knowing that he was watching her and not trusting herself to look at him.

'Suzy,' he said patiently, 'come on. Give!'

Prickles of feeling ran over her neck and shoulders. 'I don't know what you mean.'

'Oh yes you do. Tell me what's bothering you.'

'Nothing.'

'Oh for God's sake, Suzy,' he ran a hand in exasperation through his hair, 'You're about as approachable and amenable as a barracuda with tooth-ache. We were friends last night,' he coaxed.

'Yes,' she agreed dully.

'Look,' he commented reasonably, 'if we're going to be working together for the next few weeks I'd prefer it if you didn't sulk.'

'I'm not sulking,' she blazed, 'I never sulk!'

'That's an improvement. I like you better angry than sulking.'

Angry retorts leapt to her throat and were gulped down before they had a chance to surface.

'I think,' he said laconically, 'that I probably said much the same thing to Toni last night — after she'd hit me with a champagne bottle. She hadn't spoken for a whole hour before. That's quite something for Toni!'

'I shouldn't be surprised if she never spoke to you again,' Suzy flared at him, her anger splintering in her head in a shower of teasing sparks. 'That poor girl. I shouldn't think she'll ever want to *lay* eyes on you again — let alone speak!'

'You think I treated her badly?' he enquired mildly.

She stabbed her fists against the steering-wheel.

'Yes!'

'Stop vandalising my car, Suzy,' he grinned, infuriatingly refusing to be roused.

She was silent.

'In fact, I've treated Toni with exemplary restraint — the perfect gentleman personified. I think that was precisely what she was angry about. It was all rather ironic. And in the end I was even too much of a gentleman to send her packing back to Daddy and his millions. Instead I offered her the chance to cool off — in *my* villa — at *my* expense!'

'Big of you,' Suzy said contemptuously.

'Watch it!' he growled. 'My patience is not everlasting. It's very rare for me to bother to justify my actions like this. Don't push me too far with your harsh, up-tight little judgements!'

In a clanging medley of only partially understood feelings Suzy stared through her window towards the strands of waving grass and the sparkling water, but all she could see was Leon's reflection in the shiny glass. She ignored the biting criticism in his last words.

'You're telling me that you discarded a warm living person — a beautiful woman who adores you — because she wanted a little loving,' she felt herself blush at these words which seemed unduly prim and delicate, 'and you didn't feel like it — for once!'

'Loving!' he snarled. 'A gymnastic endurance test would be nearer the mark where Toni's expectations were concerned.'

Suzy did not doubt that Leon would have been well able to cope with such expectations given the inclination and motivation. Her eyes ripped forth the message through the silence.

He glanced at her derisively, his mood dark and dangerous. 'I'm the loser whatever I say aren't I, Suzy? Wrong for taking Toni to bed, cruel for refusing to.'

In a torment of rage and psychological muddle, Suzy flung herself out of the car and plunged into the under-growth which sang and throbbed with the hum of a thousand insects. He followed. She began to run. His arm went around her hips and brought her to the ground in a flying rugby tackle. He turned her over to face him. She sat up flushed and dishevelled.

'And you told me that you didn't judge, Suzy,' he reproached her. 'I thought you, of all people, would understand.'

'Understand,' she cried, 'I under-stand perfectly. Your morals and mine, Leon, are worlds apart. Bed or no bed. To me your life-style — your *love* style,' she corrected herself grimly, 'is cheap and ugly.'

She knew that her frankness would arouse his anger. She waited — was well prepared.

He said wearily, 'You can only be ugly to people who don't understand. Oh Suzy, I thought you would be different — would see that I really tried to do the best and kindest thing for Toni.'

Suzy ceased to be able to see anything now. She was past understanding anything about Leon and his women. For all she could see was him. She looked up into his face and saw genuine pain move fleetingly across it. In that moment, with sure conviction, she knew that she was in love with him, that she was like a person struck down by some terrible disease for which the cure would be long and painful.

She sighed out loud in despair. 'I don't know what to think any more,' she said with complete honesty.

His eyes grew tender. 'Suzy, there's nothing wrong with loving you know.'

'No,' she agreed in bewildered, injured tones.

'Bed is a thing of roses,' he went on gently, 'not a clump of prickles.'

'I wouldn't know. I've never been to bed with anyone,' she said, feeling that this was a terrible admission for a twenty-two-year-old to be making in the enlightened 1980s. 'I suppose you think that's touching and quaint and boring,' she challenged him.

'You're very fond of deciding what I think, Suzy.' The brown eyes glittered.

'Well — I'm right in this case, aren't I?'

'Partly.'

Suzy looked at him in the bitterest torment and realised that there had never been a man she had wanted to go to bed with. Not before Leon. Yet she knew that in spite of her old-fashioned principles and her deep-seated reticence about sex, she would have no hesitation about jumping into bed with him if he so much as twitched a long slender finger in lazy invitation. She turned away so that he would not see the naked desire in her eyes which she could feel blazing out of her like some computer read-out flashing in neon colours. She sat by the river and observed its silent inexorable movement, noticed the sunlight burning scarlet and translucent through the poppy petals which waved in the grass. He did not pursue her. The anger melted away into a pool of weariness and as the rhythmical click of crickets throbbed a lullaby in her ears she lay down in grass and slept.

It was late afternoon. He was shaking her shoulder. 'Come on, driver — I need you!' His voice was warm and kind.

'Oh,' she groaned, looking at the time, 'I'm sorry.'

For a few moments he stared at her. 'Perhaps we should both be sorry, Suzy,' he said meaningfully, 'for all that's happened in the last twenty-four hours.'

'Yes,' she replied slowly.

'Perhaps we can be friends now?' he suggested quietly.

Suzy chewed anxiously at the tip of her finger. Friend seemed an inappropriate word, not fitting their business relationship, nor yet describing any other aspect of their social and emotional transactions. One felt a comfortable liking for a friend, not the total obsession and churning desire she felt for Leon.

'Suzy,' he said softly as she stood silently before him, 'I think I understand how you feel about my love-style as you call it — and I respect your views. But . . . ' He seemed not to have the words he wanted at his disposal. She tried to help him out.

'But we have to work together,' she said with a brisk peppiness in her tone which completely belied her inner feelings. 'I'm sure we shall manage.'

He was watchful, frowning, about to speak — and then he turned swiftly and walked to the car.

Back on the road once more it was Leon's turn to slide into unconsciousness. He leaned against the head rest, his features clear and chiselled like some beautiful statue from the da Vinci period. Suzy, relaxed behind the wheel now on the gentle country roads, turned occasionally to observe her sleeping cargo, the outer shell of the man, serene in sleep. But what was the nature of the real man beneath the conflicting outer surface which could shift from fiercest anger to softest tenderness? There were many facets to consider, a variety of qualities which had been apparent in the very short time she had known him. Leon Ferrar, a man of musical talent. Leon Ferrar who commanded the respect of a hopeful young song writer who in turn described him as a strong and generous person, a man who had consideration for life's failures and unfortunates as well as the wealthy and successful. Leon Ferrar the womaniser, with a reputation as a terrific but uncommitted lover — a man who would use women to gratify his needs as and when he felt like it. Leon Ferrar who could inspire total trust and confidence, who was willing to put himself out to ensure an assistant's safety, who hid a wealth of gentleness and tenderness beneath his languid, sophisticated, controlled façade. And finally Leon Ferrar who was so wildly wantable that Suzy longed and longed for the touch of his long sensitive fingers on her body.

Suzy acknowledged this internal, moaning ecstasy of desire with total honesty, but regarded it as a weakness — something which should not happen to sensible people unless there was mutual compatibility, trust and long-term commitment to accompany it. Friends of hers had been struck by it from time to time — a strange and desperate wanting of someone else's body that reached fever proportions and caused them to behave in irrational, silly and embarrassing ways. She had also observed that the fever often departed as swiftly as it had struck and that little human warmth seemed to be left in the emotional backwash.

And now she herself had been struck down. So what was so fascinating about Leon Ferrar, Suzy wondered in a vain attempt at objectivity. Was it the man or his fame that magnetised her — or perhaps it was impossible to separate the two. The aura around the star was undeniably compelling yet Suzy sensed intuitively that there was a soft glow of warmth under that brilliant outer shining. She turned again towards Leon, felt a fresh arrow of longing deep in her breasts and thighs and pressed her lips together in exasperation. Deflecting her attention to the road ahead she attempted to imprint new images on her brain, focused her attention on the intense blue of the sky, the golden blaze of the sun and the dragonflies spiralling dizzily in the air. She marvelled at the spasmodic explosions of wild flowers along the river bank, their petals basking in the heat and the waltzing appreciation of hundreds of vivid butterflies. Driving through the little towns with their turretted churches and their timber-clad Hansel and Gretel houses, she could smell the true fragrance of rural Europe — a heady mixture of beer, freshly baked bread and dairy produce — all set against a background of flawless cleanliness: she could see it in the immaculate shop windows, the carefully tended gardens and fields, she could feel it in the clear sharp atmosphere. The excitement of being in a strange new place stirred warmly inside her.

Leon slept for two hours then woke and stretched with the suppleness of a jungle cat. He looked at the road signs, consulted the map and praised Suzy on her efficiency in making such good progress. 'But you need a rest, we'll have to find somewhere for the night,' he said thoughtfully, reaching into the glove compartment and getting out the *Michelin Guide*.

Suzy made some polite murmurings of enquiry about how far it was to Vienna.

'Oh — we should be there by tomorrow afternoon if we make an early start,' he told her.

Suzy barely heard what he said. She was more occupied with considering the implications of an overnight stop in the intimacy of a little village inn; speculating on the possible sleeping arrangements. Her thoughts and hopes lurched from crazy excitement at the prospect of being thrown together with him, through to an aching anxiety that she might run so dizzily out of control that she would never be able to piece herself together again. She pulled herself up immediately and asked herself with irritation what on earth she was thinking of! There's no question of Leon asking me to share his bed, she thought, and if he did I'd be offended that he thought me an easy lay and I'd refuse — wouldn't I? Her conviction faltered. She began to see herself as a terrible mish-mash of conflicts and indecision — a person driven by the caprice of the emotions. 'It might be a problem getting two rooms,' Leon said calmly as though he had tapped into her thoughts. 'These little village inns may be very busy in the high season.' Suzy, bright pink, held her breath and wondered what was coming next.

He commented mockingly, 'Don't worry — I'll do my best to get suitably separate accommodation and if the worst comes to the worst and we have to share I shall behave most honourably. Quite the perfect gentleman as usual,' he drawled. He was teasing her unmercifully.

Humiliation, rage and despairing longing chased frantically around her brain. 'Oh Leon, that's cruel!' she whispered.

He dealt her a look of ferocious intensity. 'No — not cruel. Clear and open and sensible is how I would describe it. You put me rather severely in my place a little while ago on this score. I intend to stay there!' His cruel, ironic derision hit her like a plank.

'Yes,' she agreed in dull submission.

'You let me know very clearly how you feel about amorous encounters, Suzy. I would not presume in any way to embarrass you more than I seem to have done already. No more skirmishes — we'll call a truce shall we?'

How could she even begin to enlighten him on the bewildering, undecipherable, paradoxical nature of her internal emotional tapestry — when she was unable to make sense of it herself. She knew that he would probably construe her silence as a passive way of agreeing with his suggestions. Her total lack of ability to communicate anything at all to him brought a blaze of hot frustration to her cheeks. She nodded in miserable acquiescence.

In the next village Leon was successful in finding two separate rooms in a delightful inn garnished with arched doorways and leaded casement windows which leaned out into the main street as though welcoming passers-by.

Suzy lay on the firm pine bed in her little turretted room, put her hands behind her head and hoped that the confusions and exertions of the day would somehow dissolve from her and melt away into the soft evening air drifting in through the windows. Gentle, comforting sounds came from the garden at the back of the inn; the chink of glasses, the ripe buzz of laughter and conversation, the sleepy chant of evening birds. She thought that she was going to like Austria.

Leon's quiet knock surprised her. 'Ten minutes Suzy. I'm starving. I'll be waiting in the bar!'

She flushed, flew off the bed, dropped her clothes on the floor where they resembled a multi-coloured puddle, and placed herself under the shower. In ten minutes she joined him, fresh and glowing.

'Hi there!' His pleasure in seeing her was unmistakable. He had ordered cool beer for her and he commanded her to dispose of it quickly so they could get down to some serious eating: fresh river trout in gooseberry sauce, salads heavily populated with fresh vegetables, black olives and nuts, sauerkraut on a side plate, hard crusty black bread — and a generous jug of ice-cold pink *Schillerwein* to help it all down.

Suzy closed her eyes in delight.

Leon, looking on with lingering approval, remarked lazily, 'I like to see a woman enjoy her food. All this dieting and self-denial is one great big turn-off.'

Suzy stabbed her fork into an olive and bristled with indignation. His habitual, casual allusions to sex were like pricks from a torturer's needle. She put on a brave, bright face.

'Well, perhaps in the circumstances I should start on a diet right away,' she responded cheerily, 'leave the contents of this plate and close my eyes so I can't see the desserts.' From the corner of her eye she sneaked a glance at the table in the corner of the room staggering under its cargo of cream-smothered *torten*, fresh fruit salad, chocolate soufflé, ripe raspberry sorbet and glistening plump strawberries, their green stalks poking up engagingly.

'Oh Suzy,' he laughed, 'you really are incredible!' He was totally relaxed now, his long body tilted slightly backwards, his mouth curved in a lazy smile. He called the waitress over, ordered Suzy a massive slice of apricot *torte* into which several ounces of nuts and cream had been miraculously trapped and gave her the wickedest of winks when it arrived.

She sighed. Her appetite had suddenly vanished. She struggled through no more than half.

Leon replenished her wineglass. 'Do you know,' he said thoughtfully, 'this must be the first time for years that no one knows where I am — not my agent, my Silver Linings colleagues, Toni, Hawk-Eye reporters, not even my mother — or indeed any other lady. Just you, Suzy. You're the only one in on the secret!'

Any other lady, she thought in despair. She looked around the dining-room and out into the garden where couples danced to the robust tones of the local brass band. Everywhere there were other ladies, pretty girls, warm attractive, desirable women. Suddenly other women had been thrown into sharp focus; she looked at them with a novel, disquieting unease. Would *that* woman appeal to Leon? Would *that* girl attract his attention? She knew now why other women would want him as she did, and so now other women began to look threatening. The feeling was new and sickening. Suzy hated it.

He reached a gentle hand across the table and touched her arm lightly, causing her to jerk so violently that she knocked her wine over. 'Hey!' he smiled, mopping up efficiently. 'I'm not that alarming, am I? I was only going to ask you for a quick dance before you collapse into bed for a well-earned sleep.'

'Oh,' she muttered, 'yes, all right.'

His style of dancing was assured, quietly authoritative and very very close. Suzy trembled in his arms as she felt the powerful thrust of his thighs against hers, as his hands gently caressed her back and shoulders, smoothing away the weariness. His breath was warm on her cheek and the smell of his skin invaded her senses. 'Suzy,' he murmured violently, 'it's damned hard to resist you.'

It was damned hard to disagree, she thought, wanting to melt into him with an urgency that almost destroyed her resolve. But she allowed the cool hand of reason to grip her. Of course Leon found it hard to resist her; there would be many others he would not find it easy to resist either. Making love was a hobby with him, a skill he worked at and polished through regular practice. And although she was beginning to doubt that he was merely a superficial womaniser she was astute and realistic enough to know that a loving tribute from Leon Ferrar did not constitute a long term emotional commitment. And that's what I want, she admitted to herself. Oh God, that's what I most want.

She disentangled herself gently, murmured good night and went to her room.

Her heart twisted with pain as she slept.

3

Suzy never felt herself to be completely in harmony with Vienna, city of music and museums, of brooding architecture and coffee houses heavy with the smell of dark chocolate. From the very first moment of their arrival, marred by the terrifying battle to get through the dense, jostling traffic of the ring-road, things seemed to go wrong. The Vienna International Hotel had no record of Leon's booking (made very carefully by her some weeks previously), which resulted in a terse exchange between him and the manager before a suitable suite was found; a suite containing a piano that is.

Leon had been tensely strung up and touchy all morning. Suzy realised that his hand was still painful and that with the passing of each day his concern about the Vienna concert was increasing. She, in turn, was tired out with the long drive in the company of a fretful passenger. She curled up on her bed and dozed off instantly. Leon came to find her.

'I've ordered lunch to be sent up here. Will you join me, Suzy please?' He was terse rather than inviting.

Obediently she got up and went to wash her face. It was, after all part of her job to keep Leon company and attempt to soothe his ragged artistic nerves.

She found him settled on a stiff, over-stuffed chesterfield in the centre of the drawing-room of the suite. She sensed that he was in one of his lazy, laid-back moods; that he wanted her to be friendly and sit next to him. As both duty and desire suggested that this would be an appropriate course of action she moved across and sat by his side. 'Is the hand still painful?'

'Yes.' He sighed. 'It just doesn't seem to get any better.'

'Can you find a doctor here in Vienna

to look at it?' she asked with quiet concern.

He smiled. 'Practical and thoughtful as ever, Suzy. I'll think about that when we've had lunch.'

He watched her pour the coffee. She felt as though a spotlight had been turned on her, making her so intensely self-aware that her skin became tinged with pink.

'It's so quiet here,' he murmured, 'so peaceful.'

'You value peace a lot don't you, Leon?'

He laughed. 'I'm in the wrong job for getting it; screaming fans, weeping girl friends, hawk-eyed journalists . . . '

'Oh, poor Leon!' She felt suddenly completely at ease with him. They sat in companionable silence, sipping their coffee and letting the tensions of the journey slip away.

He stretched with sinuous strength, his arms pulled taut behind his head and regarded her from half closed lids.

'I can feel myself getting better already,' he said, half mocking, 'approaching some state of sanity which will allow me to interpret Mozart's music. It's not just the thumb you know — it's the mind as well that has to be healthy.'

'I know,' she said softly.

'Do you really think you can manage to look after me in the run-up to this concert, Suzy?' he asked in low tones.

'Yes — of course.' Her voice was slow and serious.

'It could be hell when the day gets nearer. My God, you'll have your work cut out then!'

'That's O.K.' She felt perfectly confident. Ready for anything. There was nothing she would like to do more than look after him — and she knew that she could do it. But — if only she did not want him so much. Right at this moment she wanted to pour herself over him and leave warm kisses all over his face and neck and his wonderful strong hands. She was going to have to be very very self-disciplined, iron rigid with control.

'I know what I'd like to do,' he said

with soft purpose, so that her heart began burrowing away again in her chest like some busy, scurrying animal. 'Listen to the new album — here with you before the peace gets disturbed.'

'Oh yes,' Suzy agreed, anticipation and a curious twinge of disappointment jostling for position in her emotions.

He located the record in the luggage and slipped it on to the hi-fi equipment housed in a carved oak cabinet in the far corner of the room. The first chords of Schumann's 'Pleading Child' filtered into the room reminding Suzy of the crisp clarity of bird song in the damn stillness. She drew in her breath. Warm thrills of excitement showered down her spine. She felt as though she had been wrapped in a cloak of magic and, glancing at Leon, she knew that he felt the same strange fascination too, hearing for the first time the product of weeks of effort and concentration. She saw that his features had relaxed and that for the first time in days he was at peace with himself.

How she loved to be with him, yet how she longed to shake off this infatuation for him, stop secretly wishing that he would behave like a high-handed bastard, drag her off to his bed and make exquisite, lingering love to her. If she could stop herself wanting, she could stop the continual disappointment.

They both started in surprise and alarm as the low buzzer on the door sounded.

Leon's eyes snapped open. He sighed. 'Is there never to be just a moment's peace? Will you get it, Suzy? Try to get rid of whoever it is as soon as possible.'

Suzy went to open the door and found herself in confrontation with around five-foot nine inches of beautiful femininity dressed in azure blue silk and delicate antique jewellery. The woman smiled — the poised, untroubled smile of the wholly self-confident. 'I'm Frascana,' she said in ripe melodious tones, 'Angelina Frascana,' she continued helpfully. 'I would like to speak with Mr Leon Ferrar please.'

Suzy felt herself gaping. Frascana! The renowned concert pianist, Leon's partner-to-be in the Mozart Double Piano Concerto.

She had never seen a woman like her; such depth of loveliness, such style, such quiet understated strength — not to mention a rippling black waterfall of hair, a skin like orchid petals, a regally impressive figure and a pair of huge expressive eyes.

The night before Suzy had felt the threat of other women when she thought about Leon. The threat had been vague and confused. Now, suddenly those images fused together and formed themselves into one human form — that of Angelina Frascana.

'Come in please,' Suzy murmured, feeling that the ground was shifting beneath her.

Leon was standing at the far end of the room, a thoughtful smile of welcome on his face.

'Leon, this is Angelina Frascana,' Suzy announced gravely.

Leon smiled briefly at Suzy before fixing his eyes on Angelina and extending a hand which she took and shook warmly.

'Your agent and mine have been talking,' Angelina explained to him in a delicious Italian accent. 'He tells me that your hand is damaged, that you have had to cancel nearly all your tour, that you are taking a little holiday in Vienna to rest before our concert. Yes?'

'Yes. That just about sums it up,' Suzy heard Leon agree drily.

'Ah, I am so sorry about the hand. You see, I too am having a little holiday in this lovely city and I thought I must come to see you and find out what I can do to help.'

'That's very kind,' Leon said warmly. 'May I offer you a drink. Some coffee? Wine perhaps?'

'Oh, some wine please!'

'Suzy,' he called with kind authority as Suzy hovered at the door, wondering if she should leave the two pianists on their own, 'ring down for some wine would you?'

The wine arrived promptly together with sparkling crystal glasses on a snowy-white lace cloth. Leon dismissed the wine waiter and asked Suzy to uncork and pour the wine.

Her hands shook with emotion as she inserted the metal screw into the cork.

Angelina and Leon were engaged in getting to know each other as she placed the tray on the marble-topped coffee table.

'My English is not very good,' Angelina told him with gentle self-deprecation.

'It's charming,' Leon replied gallantly.

'Oh no, not at all. We must talk to each other in music — that will be so much better!'

'Yeah — I'm afraid I can't do much talking in music at the moment,' he said regretfully.

Suzy watched surreptitiously, her

heart struggling with envy as Angelina took Leon's hand in hers and softly stroked the injured thumb.

'Have you a good doctor here in Vienna?' she asked.

He mentioned one or two names, people recommended by his doctor in London.

'No, no,' Angelina replied with total dismissal in her voice.

'They are no good for you. You must go to my Doctor Ceccini. He is the very best in Vienna. Italian of course. I always go to see him when I am in Austria. He knows everything about a pianist's hands. I have his card here.' She held the card out in a pretty gesture of kind concern.

Leon accepted it and murmured thanks, at the same time nodding in acknowledgement to Suzy for bringing the wine.

He walked over to the table and picked up the glasses. They were tall, clean-lined and beautiful — like Angelina Frascana Suzy thought miserably.

Leon was wearing an immaculate beige linen suit with a soft camel-coloured shirt and tie. She looked at the black hair curling over his collar and the strong sun-burned fingers grasping the bottle. Desperate, desolate desire washed over her. She knew that she was no longer needed. She started to walk towards the door with the intention of going to her own room.

Leon stopped her. 'Angelina,' he said formally, 'this is Suzy Grey, my assistant. Suzy is just with me temporarily until she finds a job in teaching.'

Suzy was touched by this tactful gesture on her behalf. Angelina however, was obviously taken aback. 'Ah yes, I see,' she said vaguely, nodding briefly to Suzy with a graciously dismissive smile.

Suzy understood immediately that Angelina was well used to having servants around and that, although they would be treated with impeccable politeness they would be considered to be of little interest as people.

She retired to her room. After a while she heard the ringing sounds of the piano, its bright, sharp treble and its important bass filling the air with a rhythmical cascade of rippling notes. She imagined Angelina sitting at the piano, creating those wonderful pictures in sound — talking to Leon in music. Before a sense of loneliness and exclusion could take full hold, Leon appeared unexpectedly in the doorway. He beckoned to her with swift impatience.

'Suzy, come and listen!'

Suzy sat, as he indicated, next to him on the sofa and was instantly caught up in the brilliance of Angelina's playing. She gazed in amazement as the strong white hands flew masterfully over the keys, drawing from the instrument a truly dramatic eruption of sound. Angelina was in vibrant mood, making the piano throb to some weighty Tchaikovsky followed by some horrendously complex Chopin. Suzy noted the absorbed, appreciative expression on

Leon's face — which was only to be expected as Angelina was as formidably talented as she was elegant and beautiful. Suzy had little doubt that he would soon be irretrievably in love with her — perhaps he was already.

Angelina acknowledged their spontaneous and exuberant applause with a charmingly modest smile. 'Ah,' she mourned gently, 'such a pity we cannot play together Leon.' She lingered slightly over his name, her Italian accent sensual and caressing.

'Well,' Leon suggested, 'we could listen to some former efforts of mine.' He went to switch the elderly hi-fi on again. 'No — do stay Suzy,' he murmured as she got up hesitantly, feeling that she was now an intruder.

Angelina's eyebrows arched slightly in surprise.

The Young Listener's Album revolved on the turntable once more and the gentle sound of Brahms filled the room. It was in marked contrast to the fiery glitter of the pieces Angelina had just played and to her brilliant, showy style of execution. Suzy did not think she had heard the Brahms lullaby ever played with such tenderness. She looked again at Leon's fingers resting quietly on the arm of his chair. What sensitivity they must have in them. And what gentleness there must be in his personality to play like that for all that he could be fierce and moody and tough. The mood changed to the lively intricacy of Mozart, offered with such wit and delicacy that Suzy gave a broad spontaneous smile. She felt Leon's eyes on her, turned to look at him. His smile seemed to forge a link between them, their glances met and fused with a warm shimmer of closeness. She was glad of Angelina's presence. She knew that if she had been alone with him she would have got up and moved towards him as though jerked by an invisible thread, would have placed herself on his knee and surrendered herself to him completely.

'Mmn,' Angelina sighed lingeringly as

the last notes faded and blended into the stillness of the room, 'that was wonderful. We shall soon have you playing the really serious works,' she told him with delicious conspiracy, 'the big, big concertos,' she moved her shoulders in a sinuous gesture of expansiveness, 'Liszt — Rachmaninov!'

'Thank you. That could be an interesting prospect!' Leon's voice was dry. 'And Suzy?' he added gently, seeking her opinion.

'It was beautiful,' she said simply.

'I must leave now,' Angelina announced. She faced Leon with tender sternness in her glance. 'And you must go and see my Doctor Ceccini very soon. Very very soon!'

'I certainly will,' he smiled.

'Oh — I nearly forgot,' she laughed, 'I want to invite you to a little party tomorrow night in my hotel. Just a few friends. You will please come — yes?'

'Can I refuse?' Leon chuckled.

'No — you wicked man!' Angelina seemed to have assumed an instant familiarity with him. 'Oh — and please — if you like — bring a friend — or *amore*, a lover,' she explained suggestively.

'No lover!' he told her with a roguish smile, 'but thanks for the thought.'

'No lover,' Angelina chided with the ripe indulgent sensuality of a woman of the world. 'That is a pity. You must make love so that you can make good music — no? Especially Mozart. He loved to make love. You know that?'

His lips trembled with amusement. 'I have gathered so,' he said, 'from an inspection of the biographies.'

'Good!' she said with charming mischief. She moved her shoulders in a swift gesture of pleasure. 'Ah — we are going to get along together so well,' she exclaimed, shaking her waterfall of curls and moving swiftly down the hallway.

Suzy ran to open the door for her.

'Thank you so much,' Angelina murmured, smiling down at her. Suzy forced herself to look up, and immediately regretted it. She saw all hope of ever capturing Leon's heart recede into the violent depths of Angelina Frascana's magnificent eyes.

Stoically she returned to the drawing-room and began to collect up the glasses. Leon was slipping the gleaming new disc into its sleeve.

'Angelina is lovely,' she said dutifully, feeling that she was choking on mouthfuls of sodden gravel.

'She's one of the most sought after soloists on the concert circuit at the moment. Her technical skill is simply superb. She's a true virtuoso. A real winner,' he commented.

Suzy could well imagine. 'But your playing is so gentle, so sensitive,' she said with wistful impulsiveness, eyeing the record in his hand. He gazed at her. 'Thank you, Suzy, that's a very touching appraisal. I'm quite pleased with it myself — and I can't say that about every first pressing!' He placed the record in her hands. 'I'd like you to have it.'

'Oh no — I couldn't!'

'Oh yes you could,' he snapped. 'You do argue so, Suzy. Just do as you're told,' he growled softly, 'I don't give out autographed first pressings lightly. Consider yourself privileged!'

'Yes,' she whispered, 'I will.'

He turned away, restless and impatient again. 'I'll give this Ceccini guy a try,' he decided. 'Fix up an appointment for tomorrow morning. I'd like you to drive me, Suzy. O.K.?'

'Yes.' With an effort she matched his business-like briskness.

'Good. You can take the rest of the day off, Suzy. You must be whacked.'

Suzy swallowed, considered herself dismissed and crept away clutching her gift.

In the morning she drove him to Dr Ceccini's exclusive consulting-rooms and waited patiently outside. Within half an hour he bounded down the steps and leapt into the car looking decidedly pleased with himself. 'Seems to have been worth the visit,' he told her. 'He thinks I'll be fully operational again in a much shorter time than I even dared hope. I've got a programme of exercises to do.' He grimaced as he moved the thumb experimentally. 'There's no need to worry if it hurts like hell!'

'That's wonderful news,' Suzy grinned, catching his enthusiasm.

'Right — we'll take ourselves out on the town. Celebrate a little!'

'Oh!' She was conflicted and doubtful.

'For goodness' sake, smile. It's time you enjoyed yourself. Stopped thinking about other people's needs all the time!'

'Oh! Is that what you think?' she said indignantly.

'Yes — and I'm right! What's more it's a compliment so don't look so fierce.'

She started to laugh.

'That's better. Now just find somewhere to park this car!'

He took her to a wine bar and ordered her a delicious lunch. He was in a smiling and relaxed mood — then suddenly his eyes snapped with cold fire. 'Hell!'

'What is it?' Suzy asked in alarm.

'Over there,' he hissed. 'Do you see what I see?'

Suzy turned. With a jolt of apprehension she saw the dark brooding figure of the woman with the drooping eyelids, the same woman who had been at the hotel in Amsterdam. She was sitting in quiet watchfulness in the farthest corner of the bar.

'Hattie-Hawk-Eye!' Leon exclaimed, his face black with anger. 'My all-time un-favourite! I didn't think she'd be here quite so soon!'

'Oh dear,' Suzy said soothingly. 'Well at least she doesn't seem to have her camera with her.'

'It won't be far away. She does have to eat and drink sometimes — like other human beings. Let's get out of here before I get myself on a charge of grievous bodily harm!'

Out in the afternoon sunshine he was still tense.

Suzy was pondering on the miraculous way that this woman got to know of Leon's whereabouts and was momentarily thrown off balance when he said abruptly, 'I want you to come with me to the party tonight!'

She turned a surprised, anxious face towards him, her mind racing feverishly. 'No,' she decided firmly, 'no thank you, Leon. I'm not a friend — or a lover,' she added, recalling Angelina's words. 'I'd rather not go.'

His fingers closed in a tight circle around her arm, forming trenches in the skin. 'But I'd rather you did, Suzy,' he told her silkily.

'No!' She tried to shake herself free. One or two people looked at them curiously. A man raised a humorous eyebrow at her.

'All right then. I'm not asking. I'm telling. It's an official request. Part of your professional assistant's duties,' he informed her coolly.

Suzy recalled the night in Amsterdam, his insistence on her forming the unwanted point in a triangle with himself and Toni. 'Well,' she said, her voice dull and heavy, 'I suppose I shall have to go then.'

She looked up at him, wanted to ask what had prompted this sudden whim. But his face was closed and unreachable and she did not presume to question him.

She had to walk very swiftly to keep up with his rapid strides. Unexpectedly he stopped so that she almost collided with him. He was looking into the window of a tiny boutique crammed with canary bright clothes and flashing jewellery. A jade-green pyjama suit dominated the window, the silky material gleaming softly under the window lights.

'That's just fantastic,' he murmured.

She had to agree.

'And it's just made for you,' he said, glancing down at her with languid appraisal, his eyes taking in every line of her body.

Her face flamed and her mouth went dry.

'Will you go and try it on, Suzy?' he asked.

'No — I can't afford it,' she said stubbornly.

'But I would like to buy it for you.' It sounded like a command rather than a request.

She weakened. 'All right.'

In the tiny cubicle she wriggled into the suit, half hoping that it would not fit. But it was perfect. She loved it instantly and reflected that if Leon was going to insist on her accompanying him to the party it would certainly solve the problem of what to wear. She looked at the price tag and did some quick translation into English money. It was horrifically expensive, but she supposed that Leon could afford it. She changed back into her jeans and smoothed her ruffled hair.

'You didn't let me see it,' Leon reproached her.

'No,' she told him worriedly, 'I'll wear it tonight.'

His face became soft with tenderness. 'You're going to let me buy it for you then?'

'Yes — yes thank you very much,' she said like a polite child after a rather ghastly party.

'I can't wait to see you in it,' he drawled, taking a credit card from his pocket and settling up the account with the smiling assistant.

Suzy kept her distance from him for the rest of the day. She did not feel that she could trust herself to be with him, given her own turbulent emotions and the puzzling return of his former unpredictability. She could only assume that anxiety about his hand and the forthcoming concert was making him vulnerable and moody.

In the evening she had a leisurely bath then slipped into the suit, noticing how well it complimented her froth of newly washed hair. A little grey eye shadow and some bronze lipstick completed her preparations and she knew that the person looking back from the mirror was really quite attractive — certainly unusual. But she was hardly in the league to compete with

Angelina Frascana! She recalled the lovely oval face, the elegant tall figure, the massive violent eyes — and the generous oh-so-kissable mouth. Forget it, Suzy, she told the slender, auburn-haired reflection. Leon Ferrar is just a little intermezzo in the high summer of a rather special year.

Get ready to do without him.

She went to join him in the main room. He murmured appreciatively, treating her to one of his long, devouring looks, taking in her features, her hair, her shoulders, the rise of her breasts under the thin silk. She shivered, yet inside her was a flame of warmth. She knew yet again that if he touched her she would be powerless to resist him. But he made no gesture towards her and they proceeded correctly to the car and through the jumble of early evening traffic to the splendid luxury hotel where Angelina was staying. The sun gleamed orangey-gold over the city, touching the roofs with its gentle soft rays.

She drove carefully through the maze of one-way streets and turned into *Schwarzenberg Platz* parking in front of Angelina's hotel, the exclusive, stylish *Palais Schwarzenberg*.

* * *

Angelina's party for a few friends turned out to be a grand affair for at least one hundred guests, requiring one of the big ground-floor reception rooms to accommodate them all. Suzy faltered at the door, suddenly overwhelmed. The glittering cluster of sophisticated guests seemed to engulf her like a great, inevitable tidal wave.

Leon placed a protective hand under her elbow. 'It's O.K. I'm here!' he said softly.

Angelina disentangled herself from a little knot of guests and came to welcome them, her body moving sensuously in a draped Grecian-style gown of violet and silver. Her hair was pinned back with amethyst and pearl dragonflies so that her lovely features were all the more clearly revealed.

Leon held out a hand.

'Oh no,' she admonished with a smile, 'we greet each other like this, Italian style!' Reaching up to his face she placed her hands around it and kissed him warmly on each cheek. Then, carefully suppressing her surprise at Suzy's presence she extended a faultlessly polite hand of greeting.

They were given champagne, introduced into a laughing group of quite spectacularly beautiful people and left to be sociable. The conversation was carried out in a medley of Italian, German, French and English — the subject matter swinging from a discussion of Scarlatti's keyboard sonatas to the price of villas in the south of France. The groups of people were in a constant state of mobility, forming, splitting up and re-forming like fragments in a kaleidoscope. Suzy wished there were soft drinks available as an alternative to the champagne. She began to feel weary, her head throbbed and she was unbearably hot. Heavily engaged in listening to an English lawyer hold forth about his annual ski-ing holiday she nevertheless noticed Angelina remove Leon to another part of the room. She attended politely to the lawyer, but offered little in response so that he eventually turned to someone else. She escaped outside to the long terrace running the length of the room, overlooking the garden. The night air was humid and stifling now, the sky yellow and uneasy with the threat of rain.

'Hi there!' A handsome man with a wedge of brown hair eyed her with interest as he slouched against the terrace rail, a glass of champagne in one hand and a reserve waiting at his feet. 'You're with Ferrar, aren't you?'

'Yes,' she murmured miserably, wishing he would go away.

'Some guy. Looks like Frascana thinks so too!'

'Yes.' Her misery deepened.

'Never mind, sweetie — I'll take care of you instead. No need to feel neglected.' He moved close to her, put a hand out and stroked her cheek.

Suzy closed her eyes. The blood thundered hot and insistent in her head, yet her body trembled with an icy chill.

Her passivity was interpreted as compliance — encouragement even. The man put his glass down and wrapped his arms around her. She struggled feebly. 'Hey — you're not Ferrar's current property are you?'

'No!'

'Great — let's not waste time. Life is too short!' He began to kiss her, his mouth damp and alcohol-laden — totally unwelcome.

She did not seem to have the strength to free herself. Waves of dizziness overtook her. One moist, warm hand was on her breast now, the other massaging her bottom through the thin silk.

Without warning a third hand gripped her, a hand she would recognise anywhere, a hand of steel which pulled her roughly out of the embrace. 'Get the hell out of here,' Leon snarled to the would-be lover, flinging him away from her as though he were a stuffed puppet. Taking one look at the size and fury of his assailant, the man decided on the most prudent form of action and hurriedly melted away indoors to become absorbed in the throng.

Suzy saw Leon's face above hers, livid with anger. 'What on earth are you up to, Suzy, letting that creep maul you about?'

She passed a shaking hand over her forehead.

'You've had too much damned champagne,' Leon growled. 'You're making yourself cheap. Think how it will look!'

Suzy turned away from his fierce glare. There in the garden she saw the woman with the eyes of a hawk, her Nikon F E 2 poised and waiting — pointing in their direction. Think how it will look, he had said. How it will look! She dredged up the last vestiges of strength to confront him in hot self-defence. 'I don't care about looks,' she flung at him. 'I have nothing to be ashamed of. *My* sexual track record is faultless!'

'For God's sake, Suzy, that hawk-eye wants any dirt she can get!'

'What,' Suzy exploded, 'she surely wouldn't be interested in a little rabbit like me?'

'She's interested in *anyone*!'

'Oh really — anyone in the orbit of a star,' she shouted sarcastically.

He set his mouth grimly.

'No,' she said scornfully, 'that's not it. She's only interested in you, isn't she? You and your women. That's what she really wants!'

'Oh great,' he hissed, 'a stand-up row. Drama. She'll love that!'

Suzy glanced again at the woman. The camera was lowered. 'Well, she doesn't seem to have done much so far,' she decided contemptuously. 'She just watches.'

'She's waiting for a confrontation,' he said in an arctic voice.

'Is that what she expects from you, Leon?' Suzy asked with scorn. 'Is that what is constantly happening?'

She saw his hand twitch with threatened retaliation, then drop to his side. 'Once or twice in the past,' he said coolly.

Suzy, experiencing all the bitterness of loving which entirely ruled out any possibility of behaving with rational restraint, said with biting anger, 'You wanted me here because you think I'm a nice, sweet little rabbit. A nice little nonentity to have on your arm to protect you from the dirt seekers.'

'Damn it, Suzy,' he yelled, fury moulded onto his face like a mask, 'You couldn't have got it more wrong. When I saw that hawk-eyed female in the bar this afternoon, I knew that I needed the protection of your presence — your calmness and purity. That's what I needed.'

She hurled a contemptuous glance of disbelief at him. 'You wanted to take the dirt seeker's mind off Angelina,' she said bitterly.

'I told you what I wanted,' he snarled viciously. 'Purity and calm. But I'm getting precious little of that tonight.' He laid his hand menacingly on her neck. 'Don't spoil everything,' he warned with soft violence, 'don't spoil the beautiful picture I have of you!' He drew his breath in sharply, then turned away from her and plunged back inside, his face contorted with feeling.

Suzy collapsed against the rail. Her head blazed with dizzy heat. She realised that she must be ill, have picked up some flu bug. She needed air, needed coolness. She trudged down the stone steps into the garden where bright flowers stood suffering quietly in the thick heaviness of the evening warmth, and walked unseeingly towards the car-park beyond.

His car waited in patient silence. It looked like a long-lost friend.

But she had given Leon the keys. She could not take refuge in its smooth, cool leather upholstery.

The sky had deepened to lurid orange. It began to heave and gurgle. Warm ribbons of water came streaming down. Suzy sank to the ground, collapsing in a sodden heap against one of the car's wheels.

Her eyes closed and the hot throbbing pain in her head gradually dissolved into velvet blackness.

4

From the woodland slopes which formed a rustic garden around Leon Ferrar's Austrian villa, the view across the valley stretched over countless mountain peaks. Row upon row of them, thrusting into the sky like tightly clenched knuckles, eventually softening to a dark azure line on the horizon which Suzy found out later to be the beginning of the Italian Alps.

Now half awake in the small pine-clad room with its sloping ceiling and bleached white cotton furnishings, Suzy looked at the golden pattern of light on the blinds and felt that odd sensation of not being quite one's own person, waking in a strange place after reaching the depths of unconsciousness. Yet more new surroundings to become accustomed to, she thought hazily, and was prompted to think of actors in a play on a revolving stage, forever on the move from one set of props to another.

A rush of air set the blind bobbing against the window frame as Suzy put her legs tentatively out of bed. The dizziness had gone, although she still felt drained and weary. She raised the blind and stared curiously out of the window, noting that the air was sharp with the tang of pine needles and wild garlic, heavy with the damp earthiness of fungi growing in the dark shade where the summer sun never penetrated. Suzy realised that her room must be at the back of the villa. The garden was no more than a grassy carpet divided by a track which wound its way into the heavily wooded foot of a great mountain whose peak towered importantly way above. In the dense undergrowth hares scampered freely.

Returning to bed, she tried to sharpen up the memories of the last few hours which were blurred and smudged like a dampened ink drawing. She knew where she was, knew that she had been driven here in Leon's car. That much, at least, was clear. Other images started to leak into her mind, the feeling of being lifted gently in Leon's arms, of lying on her bed in the apartment under the stern, unbending eye of all that massive oak furniture, someone taking off her wet clothes and wrapping her in a big warm towel. And there was a face, sharp-featured, dark and swarthy, but very kind. Its owner had talked to her in a heavy continental accent whilst his hands touched her with cool professionalism and she had felt the cold rubber of a stethoscope on her back and chest. She struggled for more detail, but it was slippery and elusive like a lost dream.

There was a gentle tap on the door and Toni came tiptoeing in, her face filled with curious sympathy. 'Hi — is it O.K. to talk to you?'

'Yes — yes of course.' Suzy struggled to pull herself into full consciousness.

'Leon says you have to rest, keep real

quiet for a day or two.' Toni regarded Suzy worriedly as though she might break into pieces.

'Oh — did he?' Suzy tried desperately to remember more of what had happened.

'I'll go away if you like,' Toni said hesitantly.

'No — please stay!'

Toni smiled happily and perched on the end of the bed. Suzy stared at her in disbelief. She wore old jeans, a loose and not too clean T-shirt and very little make-up. Her eyes glowed with energy and her hair swung round her face in an untamed frizzy gold mass. She was a different girl altogether from the petulant, pouting siren who would not eat her dinner in Amsterdam.

'Suzy, it's really exciting you coming here like this all of a sudden.' Toni sounded positively cheerful about it all.

'Do you think so?' Suzy asked wearily.

'Yeah! Leon rang us — Bruno and me — at six a.m. Said you were on your way and we had to be very nice and kind to you.'

'Oh — I see.'

'You'll be just fine here,' Toni went on in rapturous tones. 'It's a fabulous place. I just love it.' She wriggled her shoulders in a shy yet coquettish manner. 'Bruno and I get on really great!'

Bruno! Suzy had forgotten all about his stay in Leon's villa. 'How is he?' she asked. 'I haven't seen him for months.'

'He's working. He works so hard!' Toni said like a proud mother.

'But he has the evenings free. He said you were at college together, but nothing heavy?' She looked at Suzy anxiously.

'Mmm?' It took a while for things to sink in. Nothing heavy! Unexpected suspicions began to trickle into Suzy's mind but she was really too tired to pursue them.

Toni smiled wistfully. 'He's writing this great song — but when he's finished he's going to start on another — just for me!'

'Ah,' said Suzy, her suspicions con-firmed.

'I'll go now. You look zapped out,' Toni said kindly. 'We have dinner at eight. Would you like it in bed?'

'Oh no, I'll get up.' She looked at her watch in amazement. It was already five-thirty. She had slept nearly all day!

'Great. See you then.' Toni wiggled away seductively, closing the door softly behind her.

Suzy sat up in bed. She was beginning to feel better already — physically at least. But emotionally she was cruelly hurt, depressed and despairing. There was a strong sensa-tion of having been banished — away from Leon's presence, from his glinting smile, his acerbic humour and his vital dark maleness. Already she missed him terribly.

On the stripped pine stool at the foot of the bed was her hold-all, thoughtfully packed with a few vital necessities. Poking from its partly zipped top was the white corner of an envelope. She slithered down the bed to inspect it further. Her name was on the front and inside was a note in Leon's strong handwriting.

'Dear Suzy', she read, 'You're to rest for a day or two, get rid of a twenty-four hour 'flu bug and general stress and strain. So Dr Ceccini tells me, and he seems to know what he's talking about. So keep calm and quiet, let Toni and Bruno spoil you — and don't you dare venture out after dark alone or you'll either get killed out there or by me! L.'

A wry smile curved Suzy's lips. The note conveyed its writer to her so strongly that she could almost feel him beside her. The intimate chiding but friendly authority of the message temporarily buoyed her up and as she dressed for dinner her good spirits began to dribble back and she was aware of feeling more than a little hungry.

★ ★ ★

Toni and Bruno were sitting together on the terrace at the front of the villa sipping chilled wine.

'Suzy!' Bruno sprang up to greet her. 'How's things? Are you O.K?'

He settled her in a chair, gave her some wine, looked concerned and protective.

'I'm fine,' she said firmly, 'please don't worry about me.'

'I think you look terrible,' Toni said with complete lack of tact but perfectly genuine sympathy. 'I can't think what Leon can have been doing to you.'

Bruno raised his eyebrows and winked at Suzy who stared stonily back. 'He certainly gave you the five-star treatment to get here,' he commented. 'Chauffeur driven in the Roller by Angelina Frascana's personal driver no less.'

Suzy stared at him. The vision of Angelina Frascana swam into her brain and completely destroyed her temporarily restored well-being. She imagined Leon and Angelina discussing her condition, arranging between them how to remove her from the scene for a short time until she regained the strength and competence to cease being troublesome and embarrassing. Leon's car. Angelina's driver. Suddenly these two special people seemed inextricably linked together, already helping each other out and operating like long-term partners.

Suzy looked at her companions and considered their collective situation, the three of them, sitting there on the terrace of Leon Ferrar's villa drinking his wine and having an idyllic sojourn at his expense. She remembered Bruno's telling her before of the procession of people lucky enough to stay at Leon's villa. She recalled with a jolt that he had jokingly referred to them as 'lame ducks'. Were the three of them just some more of these lame ducks? A spoiled heiress who needed to grow up and accept a little responsibility, a would-be song writer struggling to produce something worthwhile, an assistant who was too feeble to stand the pace of his needs and life-style when the heat was on? How far removed they all were from the talented, composed and utterly beautiful Angelina Frascana and, unlike her, how far removed they all were from Leon's presence.

★ ★ ★

'Come on, Suzy — you're not dead yet.' Bruno chided heartily. 'We'll take you out for a walk tomorrow. Fresh mountain air. It'll make a man of you!'

'Hey, Bruno. She's got to take it easy,' Toni protested.

'Nonsense,' Bruno told her cheerily. 'I've taught you to use those beautiful legs for the first time in your life and it's not done *you* any harm.'

Toni made a movement with her lips which hovered between a playful pout and a kiss.

Bruno patted her knee affectionately. 'It's true. I've taught her to walk. She's really beginning to get the hang of it — as long as I walk behind her with a whip!'

'You rat!' Toni landed a powerful punch on his chest which made him gasp.

Suzy was already becoming aware of the growing warmth between these two disparate satellites of Leon. It occurred to her that they might truly have fallen in love with each other. This tentative hypothesis was soon confirmed as Bruno proceeded to haul Toni over his knee and administer some firm but tender spanks on her delicious round bottom. She squealed and squirmed, her routine cries of protest conveying nothing but delight. Quite obviously they were in love! What on earth would Leon think, Suzy wondered, immediately realising that he would be only too pleased to pass Toni into another man's arms. It would leave his free for Angelina. She squared her shoulders in a small gesture of defiance. She could do without Leon's arms, she really could.

'Hey, we'll have to behave ourselves,' Bruno panted, returning a pink-faced, ecstatic Toni to her chair. 'Frau Becker will be here in a minute to serve dinner. She's very fierce, watches Toni and me like a bloodhound.'

Suzy learned, over an excellent dinner of fish soup, cold meats and peach soufflé, that Leon employed a formidably efficient housekeeper to look after his villa, cook the main meals and, it appeared, keep the guests very firmly in order. Although Frau Becker returned to her own house in the village each evening, it was pretty clear to Suzy that her daily presence would militate absolutely against any possibility of riotous happenings at the villa. All was order and discipline and sobriety in her domain. Stepping out of line would be unthinkable — orgies out of the question!

'I am very pleased to welcome you to Herr Ferrar's house,' Frau Becker told Suzy with stern gravity as she served the soup. 'You will please tell me if there is anything you need. Herr Ferrar likes all his guests to be comfortable.'

Toni resembled a schoolgirl bursting with silent giggles, but Suzy found Frau Becker's presence deeply reassuring, providing an air of peace and sanity which was wholly welcome. She understood that Leon's holiday villa was not a place of mindless frivolity, needless extravagance and sexual promiscuity — all of which she had previously suspected. It was a place where one could rest and reflect, where fulfilling work could be done and spiritual batteries recharged. She looked at Bruno stroking Toni's arm with his big paw and thought that if he did not produce a good song here — then he never would.

Frau Becker served coffee in the huge sitting-room, a sparsely furnished but comfortable room with beams of stout timber supporting the ceiling and plain white walls. Suzy drank hers quickly and crept off to bed, hearing the comforting tinkle of washing up going on in the kitchen below.

She unpacked her hold-all, realising that it could only have been Leon who had packed it for her, and smiling as she took out intimate items like panties and bottles of scent, flushing with wry pleasure at the thought of him touching them. At the bottom of the case was the record he had given her; that very special, personally signed first pressing. She stroked the shiny cover tenderly, looking at the picture on it with lingering interest. The picture of Leon was very recent, capturing a quite different mood from the ones she had seen before.

She gazed, giving a swift, involuntary sigh of mingled pain and pleasure. He was sitting at the piano resting his chin on his hand. His expression was reflective, wistful and tender, yet strong and full of purpose. He looked like a man to share things with, a man capable of extreme sensitivity of judgement, a man to reckon with, a man to count on. She had been so wary of him in the beginning, thinking that he would be a self-centred super-star, a man of little real worth. And then, so soon, she had fallen hopelessly in love with him. She could no longer delude herself that her feelings for Leon were simply an infatuation, a dizzy, silly crush. She loved him and wanted him more than any man she had ever known.

The picture of him was constantly in her mind's eye. She wanted to wind her arms around him and stroke away all the anger that burned inside him, experience the exquisite rapture of his arousing caresses, feel the warm sweet-ness of his tongue all over her face and body. She imagined for the hundredth time how precious it would be to have the freedom to touch him, trace every hard line and every curve of his body with her lips and tongue and fingers. Her body glowed with heat and longing. It seemed so hard that she had to come to terms with Angelina Frascana just when the threat of Toni had vanished like a bright bubble.

And how wet and useless she must have seemed to him, fainting away like that at the party like some wilting heroine in a Victorian novelette. Her despair deepened further as she reflected on the fact that she was now a liability to him — not able to work and costing him money. She resolved not to let him pay her a thing for the time she did not work. That at least she could do. She would have to think of some other way of pulling Graham out of his mess.

But worst of all was the thought that she might not see Leon for days.

★   ★   ★

In the morning she went out for a walk, taking the winding lane from the back of the villa, longing to explore the countryside; run her fingers over the spiky pine needles and dig her toes into the velvet-smooth blades of grass. Clouds of butterflies sailed into the air as she disturbed the cool peace of the thick mountain greenery. They fluttered with vigour, unlike the hazed, drugged insects which flew drunkenly between the warm petals of the sunshine-drenched flowers in the low-lying villa's terrace boxes. The infection that had knocked her out so recently seemed to have vanished, although her legs were less willing than she would have liked. And despite her precautions the relentless, ferocious sun managed to strike at her tender red-head's skin, setting it tingling with the heat. She did not stay out for long.

'Hey,' Bruno called out, inspecting her return from his comfortable seat on the verandah, 'I can see the freckles coming out in dozens!'

'Oh help!' She grinned ruefully.

'Come here,' he told her, putting down his pre-lunch beer and adjusting his navy-blue tinted sunglasses, 'I've something to show you.'

He flourished a copy of a day-old English newspaper, freshly collected from the village shop. 'Look there,' he said, pushing it under her nose.

Suzy looked. On the front page was a picture of Leon and Angelina, smiling into each other's eyes. The caption underneath was headed with the words, 'Romantic Overtures', and went on to inform the readers that Leon Ferrar, well known for his reticence about his various lovely ladies, had declined to make any comment on being the guest of honour at the beautiful Angelina Frascana's glittering party held in a luxurious Vienna hotel — etc, etc. Suzy's eyes skimmed rapidly over the predictable phrases. There were a number of allusions to the possibility of a flowering romance between the famous, but very differently talented pianists; suggestions to the effect that they might be 'two in harmony' and eventually concluding with the speculation that perhaps the famous Ferrar and Frascana might be embarking on a relationship which could be a 'duet for life'.

Suzy handed the paper back to

Bruno with a certain grim despair.

'Umm, 'duet for life' — I wonder about that,' he mused, 'nice work if you can get it. She looks a pretty classy lady!'

Suzy murmured in assent.

'I reckon they could be well suited,' Bruno continued, his cruel persistence in pursuing this painful topic entirely unintentional. 'A bit up-market for my taste though,' he grinned, watching Toni wiggle out on to the terrace, her hour-glass figure displayed to full advantage in a clinging low T-shirt and the briefest of cotton shorts.

Bruno was quite right on both counts, Suzy judged. Angelina was right out of his class and she was, of course, ideally matched to someone of Leon's calibre. Suzy perceived, in a trembling thrill of enlightenment, how Angelina and Leon would be natural allies, two vital, elevated and exotic people unintimidated by the world, supreme and assured, filled with purpose and confidence and vigour. Leon she now saw as completely unattainable. Angelina was quite simply his sort of woman — a rare and superior being who would expect a man of equal supremacy — and have no trouble in getting him!

'Super, isn't it,' Toni exulted, taking up the newspaper and reading out one or two choice lines from the article, inflicting further torture on Suzy's raw emotions. 'I'm sure glad he's found someone nice so he won't be fretting about me now I'm concentrating on Bruno!'

Suzy noted the ingenuous, harmless vanity in her voice and thought that Leon had had a lucky escape. Much as she warmed to Toni's spontaneous, child-like friendliness, she understood entirely now why he had been so desperate to shake her off.

They went inside to eat Frau Becker's excellent cold lunch which had been left out on the big pine table in the dining area. Frau Becker had unobtrusively but meticulously tidied the villa and had now returned to her own home until the early evening when she would return to cook the supper.

'Hey Suzy, there's a party on tonight,' Bruno announced, sinking his teeth into a vast apricot, 'You'll come with us, won't you?'

'What party? Am I invited?'

'Yeah — sure. It's open house at Tom Allen's place down the road. Rich Yank, friend of Toni's. She met him in the village. What a coincidence: they're almost neighbours in California. It'll be a great do — barbecue, big fat steaks, loads of free booze. Fantastic!'

Suzy laughed at his exuberance. He was a great big lovable darling. She recalled Leon's instructions to keep calm and quiet. With a sudden upsurge of rebellion and self-assertion she exclaimed brightly, 'Yes — why not? I'd love to come!'

'That's real neat,' Toni exclaimed, 'We'll have a great time — all three of us!'

Suzy sighed inwardly. She seemed to be cast in the leading gooseberry role at the moment.

As soon as possible after lunch she escaped to her room and abandoned herself to the luxury of some solitary moments of self-pity. She glanced in the mirror and grimaced at the mess the sun had made of her delicate white skin. When she slipped her shirt off there was a livid triangle on her throat and chest — like an upturned road sign in the snow. She would have to be careful. It would be just too bad to get sunstroke on top of everything else and be totally useless for the rest of her time in Leon's employ.

She lay on the bed and dozed lightly.

Toni came to wake her a little later. She had two dresses over her arm. 'I thought you might not have anything to wear tonight,' she said, with her usual brand of utterly well meant tactlessness.

Suzy wondered what made people want to give her clothes! She supposed that in contrast to the glamorous people she was currently mixing with, she appeared a little dull, with that unmistakable air of dressing on a shoe-string.

The dresses were beautiful and exclusive — if not quite her style. One was in emerald green silk, slit up to the thigh. The other was black and gauzy — a real party frock with a mass of intricate crisscrossed straps on the bodice. Suzy knew that they must have cost a fortune and also knew that Toni genuinely wanted to give them to her in a totally spontaneous gesture of generosity. She was touched. 'They're just lovely, Toni,' she said, 'I'll be really pleased to have them. Thank you.'

Toni beamed. 'You could wear the green one tonight — and I've got a lovely clip for your hair. I'll put it in for you.'

So later on Suzy put on the green dress and allowed Toni to fuss with her auburn curls. She brought two clips made from diamonds and emeralds and caught Suzy's hair up high above her ears with them. The effect was very striking. Suzy pulled a thin gold belt tightly over the dress then bloused the spare material over it to adjust it to a suitable length. The slit showed a good deal more of her rounded white thigh than she would have liked but she decided not to worry about it. A thickish layer of sunblock toned down the brightness of her nose and cheeks and on Toni's advice she completed the effect with glistening green eye-shadow and bright coral lipstick. She looked in the mirror and felt a mingling of surprise and alarm. She was used to seeing a clear, open, girlish face looking back, but tonight she saw a young woman.

A young woman who could perhaps be daring and assertive, who might not be wholly predictable in her behaviour.

Whoever you are, she thought, staring at the image, you're not the little rabbit Leon Ferrar used to think he saw. Automatically her mind raced to consider what he would think of her now. She still ached for his presence. She wished he was here now to take her to the party — or *did* she? Wasn't it time to stop yearning for Leon, stop being miserable, stop wallowing in self-pity — and start living again. What did it matter what he might think of the enticing, provocative Suzy Grey smiling back from the mirror. She was her own person — strong-minded enough to do as she pleased without concern for anyone's approval — even his! And what better time to start than tonight.

* * *

Flanked between Bruno and Toni, Suzy looked up at Tom Allen's big log cabin and was reminded of fairy-tale stage sets in pantomimes when jolly barons appeared with their pretty daughters and sang with more enthusiasm than musical skill. The cabin had a high pointed roof with overhanging eaves and decorative timber work over the big, shuttered windows. Evening sunshine filtered through the thick slats. The garden was looped around with a necklace of gaily-coloured lanterns, bobbing gently in the soft breeze. Guests chatted and relaxed on the grass where tables and chairs were liberally scattered. In the far corner of the garden a huge barbecue crackled and hissed under the weight of dozens of cutlets and steaks and sausages. At regular intervals it puffed up curls of white smoke into the air — making it seem like a live thing — a snorting yet fully domesticated dragon.

'Any friend of Toni's is a friend of mine,' Tom Allen said affably, looking Suzy over with an experienced and approving male eye. 'Do you drink champagne?'

'Well — sometimes!' Suzy's eyes sparkled with mischievous anticipation.

'It's the only thing worth drinking in my opinion,' Tom told her, pouring a golden froth of cooled wine into a huge bronze goblet. 'There, get that down you. You young lovelies are all far too skinny. Same goes for Toni!'

'No, I'm far too fat,' Toni giggled happily.

Bruno patted her shapely bottom. 'In all the very best possible places, Toni baby!'

Tom Allen moved away. There were many other guests for him to consider.

It was a big, expensive, exuberant party. Toni watched him. 'Attractive guy, isn't he?'

'Hey,' Bruno chided, 'I'm jealous!'

'Don't be,' Toni said sweetly, turning her most appealing glance on him. As she emerged from his gorilla-like embrace she grinned slyly at Suzy. 'You know I think you've made a hit with Tom. He's a great guy, he really is.'

'Bit ancient though,' Bruno snorted dismissively.

'No,' Toni disagreed, 'he's only mid-thirties. It's just because he's going bald that he looks kinda old.'

Bruno was unconvinced.

'He's real nice,' Toni continued, eyeing Suzy with heavy thoughtfulness. 'He spends half his time here and half in California. He does computers or something — has a firm in Munich. He's on the look-out for a new wife as well!'

'What happened to the old one?' Suzy smiled.

'Oh — I dunno. They're divorced; who isn't?' Toni's feet were tapping impatiently to the rhythm of the 1960s' Beatles' hits coming from the big speakers on the verandah. 'I wanna dance,' she pleaded huskily, gazing up at Bruno.

'See you, Suzy!' Bruno swept Toni away and they joined the laughing, throbbing throng on the flat grassy space which served as an idyllic under-the-sky dance floor.

Suzy wandered around on her own. The atmosphere was low-key and relaxed. She felt perfectly at ease and soon joined one of the friendly, laughing groups. They were local people who spoke as much English as she did German. She suggested that they tried some halting French and with the aid of some vigorous gestures and the consumption of considerably more champagne they were soon communicating very happily.

For supper Suzy had steak, sausages and wafer-thin chips together with a number of special relishes which Tom had specially imported from the States. Then there were flavoured ice-creams, hot waffles and syrup and fruit tarts. She began to thoroughly enjoy herself. She found that she was giggling a good deal for no particular reason. Other people seemed to be doing the same. It was a great party.

One or two young men, of varying nationalities asked her to dance, then unexpectedly Tom Allen cut in on one of them. 'Excuse me,' he said, 'a host's privilege.' He moved gently and rhythmically putting his arms around her lightly. 'Enjoying yourself, sweetheart?' he asked.

'Mmm — yes.'

He questioned her on her family, her job, her background, her tastes in food and books and music. He was very courteous but unmistakably predatory. He was a very special man, Suzy had to admit, but not the one for her. She could never do more than just like him. The chemistry wasn't there.

She emitted a little giggling hiccup.

'Hey — baby, you've been hitting the champagne. Want to go and lie down?'

'Oh no — don't want to miss the fun!'

He had to leave her soon. He was a good host — paid attention to all his guests. But Suzy saw him watching her; through the singing, humming haze in her head she saw his eyes appraising her body with shrewd purpose.

Around midnight she went into the house to find the loo, then splashed cold water on her cheeks and forehead. Her face in the mirror looked flushed and wild.

Tom Allen was on the landing staring pensively at an abstract painting hung on the wall. 'Hi,' he greeted her — 'like it?'

'Yes,' she giggled again. 'I do like it. I

think I like everything tonight.' She looked up at him, noting the tanned skin, the rug of brown hair covering his chest revealed under a shirt that was open to the waist. His arms were hairy too and strongly muscled — and the glance of invitation from his hawkish blue eyes was undeniably compelling. He was an athletic and powerfully sexual man. Through the pleasant haze of the champagne Suzy felt him exert a little magic over her.

Her sexual inexperience had never bothered her before. Now suddenly she wished that she had one or two lovers to reflect on. She was a girl with no past. That was beginning to seem dull rather than virtuous. Was this a good opportunity to alter the situation?

He was watching her carefully. She allowed him to take her arm. 'I sure would like to show you my house,' he said, pulling her gently towards a door at the end of the dark wood-panelled corridor. On the other side of the door was a big panelled bedroom furnished solely with a massive bed covered with a deep maroon and black Spanish cover and a small table with drinks and glasses.

'My sleeping den,' he said, 'nothing happens in here — except bed!' He raised his eyebrows in unmistakable invitation.

Suzy's impulse of a few minutes before evaporated as swiftly as it had developed. 'Tom,' she said with as much dignity as possible, 'you're a lovely man but I don't want to go to bed with you. We London students don't go to bed with everyone you know,' she went on trying to look stern as she rocked a little on her feet, 'whatever the papers say!'

'Is that really so?' he grinned, unperturbed. He wrapped his arms around her and nuzzled her hair. The clip caught a little painfully on a trapped strand. She felt him easing down the zip fastener at the back of her dress, stroking her skin. The caress was not unpleasant.

'Tom,' she chided, 'that's not fair!'

'No, sure — you're right. Not cricket at all as you English would say,' he joked. His fingers were creeping down the small of her back, reaching into the lace panties, stroking the roundness of her buttocks.

'Tom, let me go — please,' she whispered.

He released her immediately. 'O.K. No hard feelings?'

'No.' She meant it. He was a very nice man even if he was an expert and casual seducer. She knew that he would never have forced her and that he would have been a superbly gentle lover if she had been willing. She wished in some ways that she could have wanted him — freed herself from the torment of wanting Leon for a while. The garden was dark now. Toni and Bruno had disappeared. The guests were mainly lying on the grass in affectionate tangles — chatting or nibbling at each other. The food was finished but the champagne continued to flow. Suzy located her goblet. It was full again! She saw Tom, dancing now with a tall blonde Austrian girl. His hands were squeezing her buttocks as he murmured softly in her ear.

Suzy smiled to herself. The champagne and the warmth fused together in her brain. She was very drowsy. She sat on the soft grass with her back resting against a pine tree.

* * *

As she opened her eyes she found herself in confrontation with a long expanse of cream-trousered leg. Her eyes travelled upwards over powerful thighs, slender haunches, a broad chest and strong wide shoulders. There was an insistent, violent pounding in her head as she met Leon's dark eyes — penetrating hers with snapping golden brown fire.

'Good morning, Suzy.' She could hear the tight angry contempt behind his icy politeness, yet the mere sound of his voice sent her blood leaping on some frantic journey around her veins.

'Hullo.'

'You look a little rumpled,' he remarked. 'Are you still intact?'

She shook her head defiantly, then wished she had not. It felt as though a heavy weight were thundering about inside it.

'What time is it?' she asked stupidly. 'Why are you here?'

'Three o'clock. Time we were going home.' He reached out a hand and as she took it pulled her roughly to her feet. She swayed. He fastened an arm of steel around her, digging his fingers ferociously into the flesh of her upper arm.

'You're hurting,' she complained.

'Good,' he said silkily, smiling a polite greeting to an entwined couple who were sitting nearby. No one would have guessed, as they walked along together, linked closely, that they were not idyllic lovers.

Suzy tried to wriggle away.

'Stop it,' he growled softly. 'It won't do any good. I'm trying to extricate you from this place with a shred of dignity still left.'

Suzy began to giggle again. 'I'm on holiday,' she told him. 'It's my night off.'

'My God — the minute I leave you alone, you're either flirting with hunks of virile muscle, trying to get yourself raped or drinking yourself silly!'

'Mmm,' she chuckled, 'I bet Angelina doesn't get tight.'

He stared at her — his eyes brilliant with fury. 'Leave Angelina out of it,' he snapped. He opened the passenger door and flung her roughly in.

'Ooh — you can drive again!' She collapsed in a heap.

'Yes,' he said grimly, 'I can do *everything* again.' He started the engine.

She patted her hair. With a horror which brought back a little sobriety she realised that one of the clips was missing. 'Oh help!'

'What is it?'

'Don't go. I've lost one of Toni's clips. It's diamonds — precious. I've got to find it.'

He switched off the imperceptible purring. 'Where the hell is it?'

Suzy creased her forehead, trying desperately to put her brain in some kind of working order. In a flash of recall she was standing again in Tom Allen's bedroom feeling the hairs tighten as he nuzzled her. He must have dislodged a clip.

'Oh God,' she moaned.

'Well,' Leon asked with glacial anger, 'do we have to search the bushes and woodland lanes?'

'No,' she said quietly, 'it's in the house.'

'I'll get it. You're in no fit state.' He was swinging himself out of the car. 'Where do I look?'

Suzy closed her eyes in despair. How on earth was it going to seem to Leon when she told him where the clip was likely to be?

'Well, come on, hurry up, Suzy. I was hoping to get some sleep tonight.'

'It's in the main bedroom — I think.'

She saw a muscle move in his jaw. He said nothing and strode away towards the house. Numb with misery Suzy leaned her head against the rest and closed her eyes. The world whirled and sank in spinning blackness. She sat up again sharply realising how much the wine had affected her. But it did not prevent her following Leon in her mind to Tom Allen's room, guessing at the passionate scene he might find there with Tom and whatever girl he had eventually found to share his bed. What a dreadful position to put Leon in on top of everything else.

★　★　★

She slunk down into the seat and wished she could vanish. He returned almost immediately, tossed the clip into her lap and turned the ignition key viciously. The car's quiet power took

152

them effortlessly along the winding valley road and up the steep slope towards the villa.

There was a stopping place for picnickers under the trees. Leon pulled in sharply and switched off the engine. The first traces of dawn were already showing on the velvety dark horizon. Birds were singing with sharp chiselled notes.

Suzy glanced at him nervously. 'Where are Toni and Bruno?'

'Came home hours ago. They looked everywhere for you — thought you must have got a lift with someone else — or decided to stay on.' He looked grim and dark and unreachable.

She sensed that he had stopped in order to remonstrate with her out of earshot of the villa. A bright spark of anger kindled inside. What crime had she committed that he should presume to take her to task. 'I've been enjoying myself — that's all. I've done nothing terrible and you've no need to look at me like that,' she told him, stung by the revulsion and contempt she read in his eyes.

'Oh no?' he queried acidly, 'no need to be disappointed that the girl I thought so clear and sparkling and pure could make herself look so cheap!'

'Cheap!' Rage splintered in her head. 'You bastard,' she exploded; she, who had never before in her whole life sworn at a man; at anyone. 'You have no idea what has gone on.'

'I've a very good idea,' he remarked, dark with anger.

'And even if you had,' she spat at him, 'my private life has nothing to do with you. Just leave me alone!' How bitter it was that he should think she was used to behaving like a little tart — a trollope.

He gripped her wrists and pinned her back against the seat. She was suddenly strong and managed to writhe from his grasp.

She faced him with fierce determination. But before she could speak her stomach began to lurch. She felt distressingly queasy. She flew out of the car and plunged into the dewy dampness of the trees, then stood, bent over clutching her stomach with both arms. Saliva juices poured into her mouth but she was not sick. Straightening up she gulped in deep breaths of the sweet morning air and felt astonishingly revived.

He was standing behind her.

'Are you all right, Suzy?' His voice was soft and tender.

'Yes.' She kept perfectly still.

His body was so close to hers that she could feel the movement of his ribcage as he breathed. His arms moved around her, holding her under her breasts.

'Don't,' she whispered fiercely. 'Don't.' She could not bear for him to be so near and yet so finally unattainable.

His arms dropped away. 'It's that other man you want, is it?' he asked with sweet mockery. 'Or perhaps you've already had your fill of masculine attentions. Had sufficient for one night?'

'How dare you sit in judgement on me like some god?'

His face had that look of careful, menacing control that she had seen on their very first meeting. His strong fingers shot out and gripped her shoulders. He touched the soft green material with lingering assessment.

Her eyes blazed up at him. The more control he demonstrated the more the anger swelled inside her until it had to break forth. 'I suppose you disapprove of my appearance as well,' she flung at him.

His eyes narrowed dangerously. 'No, not at all. Quite the opposite. You look — ravishing.'

She knew he had chosen the word deliberately. 'Well no one has ravished me, Leon,' she warned defiantly, tossing her curls slightly. 'Isn't that a waste?'

'Oh yes,' he agreed, quietly — 'a terrible waste!' His hand moved to the clip which remained in her hair. 'So he didn't put his fingers through your hair,' he asked softly caressing the warmth of her skull with a tender violence which made her tremble. 'He didn't move the zip at the back of your dress — which you forgot to do up.' His other hand was wrenching at the tell-tale fastener. 'You're not just a little flirt after all?' She could feel the menace now in the hardness of his body against her. She told herself to wriggle away but his hands were on the bare flesh of her back awakening instant trails of desire which spread through her hips and thighs.

He laid his lips on hers and silenced any further protest. His mouth was alternately hard then sweet and yielding. He teased and explored with his tongue — gentle, slow and delicate. He seemed to be drawing the life from her. She was falling into exquisite oblivion, sinking into a warm, caressing sea of softness.

'Was *he* any good at kissing,' he asked sarcastically, pulling away from her a little, 'a man who can't kiss can't make love either you know?'

Suzy felt that he was squeezing the life from her heart. He was punishing her in the time-honoured way of a man who knows far too much about women. Yet again she had allowed him to entice her halfway down the winding path leading to ecstasy and seduction. The bitterness of his sophisticated playfulness twisted into her heart like a stone-whetted blade, for she still loved him — quite terribly.

'Stop it,' Suzy moaned, reaching in futile despair for the zip fastener and her self-respect, 'Please stop it. I don't want you to. Please!'

★ ★ ★

She stumbled to the car. He followed. Got in. Restarted the engine. He was silent.

'Leon,' she told him, her voice calm and sure. 'Don't ever do that again, please. I can't bear it.'

His features stiffened. He gave a deep sigh and ran a hand through his dark hair. He turned away from her slightly. His strong shoulders seemed to droop. In any other situation — with any other man Suzy would have concluded that she had inflicted a deep wound. But this morning — with Leon — she was aware only of her own pain.

5

Suzy pulled herself from the tendrils of drugged sleep as her bedroom door opened and Leon strode in. He handed her a cup of strong hot coffee then sat on the edge of the bed and inspected her critically. 'Well,' he asked softly, 'how fit do you feel?'

She straightened up. 'Fine,' she stated with conviction. It was almost true. A pint of grapefruit juice and some aspirin before she slept had done wonders for her head. His eyes were sharply appraising and her heart began to speed up as she met his gaze. She had forgotten how wonderfully attractive he was, how powerfully built, how languidly strong; his thick hair midnight blue and shiny and his skin a shade of olive-gold. His shrewd eyes remained watchful under slightly lowered lids.

'I sent you to my villa to rest,' he commented drily, 'but as you seem to be determined to exert yourself — you might as well come back with me to Vienna and exert yourself to some purpose — on my behalf!' His mouth was stern but his eyes betrayed a flicker of amusement.

Joy zipped through her veins. Life was suddenly worth living again. 'Yes — yes,' she agreed enthusiastically, 'I'll be ready as soon as you like.'

He reached out a hand and laid it gently for a moment on the side of her face. She said anxiously, 'Leon — about last night . . . '

'Forget last night,' he cut in swiftly, 'don't remind me about it.' He got up with an impatient movement and looked down at her with detached assessment. 'Five minutes?' he enquired coolly, 'well, perhaps ten!'

Suzy knew that he would not be joking. Although she was not quite sure which part of last night he had wanted her to forget — she was perfectly sure that he wanted to be off as soon as possible.

She jumped out of bed and started to move fast.

A quarter of an hour later, Toni and Bruno, heavy-eyed and yawning, were waving them off with sleepy surprise.

Leon rammed his foot hard on the accelerator. 'I've got a lot of lost time to make up for,' he informed Suzy as they sped towards Vienna on the west-bound autobahn. 'It's time to get down to some serious work. My hand is almost better, Toni is safely occupied and happy — and you seem to be back to your normal self, thank God! What's more Hattie-Hawk-Eye has gone back to London clutching her trophies and probably all set to torment some other poor devil.'

Suzy winced, recalling the scoop photo of Leon and Angelina in its prominent page one position. A trophy indeed!

'I need to be at the piano constantly,' he continued, 'you're going to be on permanent stand-by — cups of coffee, the odd whisky, lots of moral support, keep all visitors away and protect me from the telephone. Will you be up to it?' His tone was alarmingly brisk.

'Yes. Of course.' He had reverted, she noticed, to the cool affability which enabled an employer and employee to work comfortably at close quarters. The Schlezbruck incident seemed to be firmly out of conversational bounds.

'Is your hand really better?' she wondered.

'It still hurts,' he said matter-of-factly, 'but I can play the piano without any trace of handicap. Angelina's miracle doctor gave me drugs and massage and decreed that the hand should be used.'

'It was a stroke of luck to find out about him,' Suzy volunteered with an effort as she struggled with the pain of Angelina's beautiful image once again.

He gave an assenting nod. 'This concert's getting terrifyingly near. I hope I can keep sane!'

'I'll help you keep sane,' she told him as brightly as she could manage, 'I really think I'm well enough to cope — even with you!' she added mischievously, longing to make some warm contact with him, to break out of the correct professionalism which pulled them apart. She waited for the languid turn of the head, the lazy smile, the sardonic, 'I'm sure you can cope, little rabbit,' — but it never came. She pressed her lips together and tried to be rational and mature about the hurting going on inside her.

★ ★ ★

There were two letters for her at the hotel; one from her mother with encouraging news of her father's good progress following his illness and chatty little details of day-to-day English life that made her momentarily engulfed with homesickness, the other from Graham which was somewhat less cheering. For some time Graham had been working for Rod Slater, a local garage owner, in order to earn a little extra cash. Graham was only seventeen, still at school and constantly causing problems for himself through his heavy-handed carelessness. On one occasion he had broken a windscreen wiper off a customer's car whilst washing it and on another dented a bonnet when he dropped a hose-pipe on it.

In the past Suzy had helped him out with gifts of money and small loans to make right the damage he had done. But as she read the letter today her heart sank. This time things sounded even more serious than she had anticipated. This time Graham really had overstepped the mark — taken Rod Slater's own Porsche 911 out for a little 'test drive' after washing and polishing it. There had been a confrontation with a kerbstone and a lamp-post. 'Looks bad Suzy,' the letter said, 'I wasn't covered for insurance and the damage looks like a few hundred quid. Slater says it won't be necessary to tell the police if I can stump up the cash. He's threatening to tell Dad, but I've held him off so far. I'm going through hell thinking up ways to pay. Might have to tell Dad soon. Hope not. But don't you worry about it, Suzy. You've done enough already. Have a ball — flirting with Ferrar and swanning round in the Bentley. Lucky you. I'm dead jealous.

Love G.'

Oh Graham, she thought, when you grow up you'll learn that you can't tell people things if you don't want them to worry.

A few hundred pounds. She would never be able to give Graham that sort of money. She stood staring at the paper, her mind searching furiously for solutions, her emotions bleak.

Leon was standing in the doorway of the drawing-room, silent and watchful. 'Bad news?' he queried.

She jerked herself up straight. She

did not want to burden or irritate him with her family's problems. 'No, no,' she said brightly, 'just routine news from home. They're all fine.'

He raised an eyebrow, shrugged and walked away to start on some serious work at the piano.

Recalling his instructions, Suzy made coffee and took it into him. He nodded in brief acknowledgement but did not take his eyes from the complex score in front of him. There was a look of fierce concentration on his face as though he were somehow detached from everyday existence and lost in the music. Suzy crept away and stood outside the door listening entranced. Suddenly the rhythmic ripple of notes ceased. She heard him muttering to himself. 'Suzy,' he shouted.

She jumped in surprise, went to him immediately.

'There's no need to lurk behind the door,' he growled. 'If you want to listen you can sit in here. It won't bother me. I won't even notice you.'

'Oh!' She tried not to feel terribly hurt.

'I don't notice *anything* when I'm playing,' he said. 'Toni could never understand that. She used to take it as a personal insult. But it wasn't.' He looked through the musical score, creasing his forehead. 'Find my pen will you, Suzy,' he requested abstractedly.

'I think it's in the pocket of the black leather jacket — in my room.'

Suzy opened the heavy oak wardrobe, pulled the leather jacket from the others hanging there and laid it on the bed. Her hands shook a little. To be in this room where Leon's things were lying around, sweaters over an armchair, ties and cufflinks on the dressing-table, hair brushes, cheque cards and bottles of aftershave, brought the powerful essence of the man to her in the most subtle yet dramatic way. Resisting the impulse to stroke the fabric of the suits in the wardrobe and evoke memories of the wonderful smell of his skin by sniffing at the aftershave, she slipped her fingers into the pocket of the leather jacket. There were two pens inside; one the black fountain pen she had seen him use often, the other a slender, elegant silver ball pen. There was also a business card. She could not resist taking it out and having a look. Her chest reverberated with shocked curiosity. The card bore Angelina's name with her Rome address and phone number on the front in violet lettering. On the back was a message — the handwriting stylish and graceful. 'Leon, *caro* — please feel free to call anytime if you should need me. Do I need to say more!'

Suzy stared at those innocent yet intimate words and her spirits dribbled away like the remnants of an ice lollipop on a warm day. She wanted to creep into a dark little hole and howl! Of course she had known all along about Leon and Angelina — it was just that the written message brought things rather brutally home. She took him the fountain pen.

★ ★ ★

The time crept on.

★ ★ ★

'Suzy,' he called abstractedly, 'would you order a meal to be sent up here in an hour or so. I don't want to break off to dress and go down to the dining-room.'

'Yes, of course,' she reassured him.

'And I'd like you to eat with me,' he went on. 'I need company to help me unwind when I've been practising.' The request hovered between a warm invitation from a needy friend and the formal instruction of a boss. Whatever his motive, Suzy found herself over-joyed at the prospect of spending time on her own again with Leon — talking, watching, adoring — accumulating some assets to put in her memory bank for the time when he would no longer be in her life.

'I'll choose you the dinner of the month!' she smiled.

She went down to the dining-room and consulted the extensive menu, spending time and care in selecting all the things that Leon would especially enjoy. She then asked for the wine list and ordered the Chablis he frequently chose for himself, giving instructions that it should be well chilled. When the food and wine arrived she sent the staff away and set to work arranging the meal on the table as attractively as possible.

Leon remained oblivious to her, fully occupied on the piano in the far corner of the big room.

The door buzzer sounded. Suzy went to answer it anticipating that something for the dinner had been forgotten. But instead she found Angelina standing outside, lovely, composed and smiling. Suzy found herself gaping. She quickly pulled herself together. Leon had said no visitors but she was sure that Angelina would be an exception.

Angelina was dressed in a sky-blue silk dress with gold and white appliqué on the wide sailor style collar. Her legs were bare, their pale golden tan shown off to perfection in gold high-heeled sandals. She had taken her hair back from her face so that the high cheek-bones were visible. It seemed to Suzy that Angelina had used the time since she had last seen her for the sole purpose of growing more beautiful. How could one even begin to compete with all that loveliness?

Give in now! Suzy told herself. But loving Leon was not some kind of race where she had to run against other women, like greyhounds after a hare — was it. Loving him meant just that. Being prepared to love and care about him whether or not he cared for her or preferred her above someone else. That was real loving. But was she strong enough to make do with that; to love him without getting anything in return.

She supposed that she would have to be; she did not think there would be any alternative.

Angelina progressed into the room in a haze of jasmine-based perfume and Suzy trotted behind in a great wet squelch of misery. Leon was still playing.

Angelina tilted her head so that the mahogany-dark curls rippled in a shiny velvet waterfall across her shoulders. She listened intently, then smiled, revealing a flash of even white teeth. 'He's doing wonderfully,' she smiled, 'fantastic. *Dolce, tenoro, supplichevole* — that means — tender, appealing,' she added helpfully to the watchful Suzy.

The piano was suddenly quiet. Leon turned around. He looked tired and rumpled. He stared uncomprehendingly at Angelina like someone waking from a deep sleep. Delighted recognition lit up his features.

She advanced on him, gave him her warm Italian kisses of greeting then said, 'I think you have forgotten our appointment you wicked man!' Her voice was ripe with gentle indulgence.

He stared. 'Yes — oh God, yes!'

'Supper at the Aubergine.' She pronounced the word with soft Italian charm — 'ooh-bear-sheen'. Her tone remained sweetly chiding.

'Eight-thirty?' she queried teasingly, 'I've brought my Alfa Romeo to take you in style!'

'Oh hell,' he groaned. He glanced hesitantly at Suzy, his face a mixture of apology and irritation.

'It's all right, it doesn't matter at all,' she lied, her voice stiff with the effort to hide disappointment.

'Oh Leon, you have let Suzy order dinner. You really are a wicked man!' Angelina smiled soothingly at both of them. 'But I'm sure this lovely food will not go to waste. Suzy will be very hungry after looking after you.'

Having effectively demolished Suzy's efforts, her composure and her entire evening, Angelina turned her full attention to Leon whose face displayed a mingle of fatigue, exasperation and contrition. He threw Suzy a glance of pure appeal — an expression she had not seen him wear before. 'Hell,' he muttered, 'I'll be ready in a few minutes.'

'Oh dear,' Angelina smiled as he vanished into his room, 'I shall have to be very careful with him. I'll soon have him looking happy again,' she decided with impregnable confidence.

'Yes,' Suzy murmured, 'I'm sure you will.' She did not doubt that Angelina would have a few sure-fire ways of making Leon happy.

She invited Angelina to sit down and brought her a glass of chilled wine in a crystal goblet.

'Thank you so much,' she smiled taking a lingering, regal slip. Leon soon joined her. As they were leaving, he hovered at the door. Suzy knew that he was feeling guilty, regretting his forget-fulness and her wasted efforts. She hated to feel a burden like some dull, boring relative who needs to be humoured.

She sensed a restraint in him as Angelina stood beside him, dark and statuesque like some Renaissance goddess.

Suzy smiled, stretching her lips tight to stop them trembling with emotion. 'Good-bye,' she said with brittle cheeriness, wishing that she could cling to Leon, prevent him from leaving her. 'Do you want me to pick you up in the car later on?' she asked correctly.

'No, no,' Angelina waved a dismissive hand, 'I shall bring him home safe and sound myself.'

Leon stared down at Suzy, momentarily stripped of his sardonic control. 'Suzy,' he said in a low voice, 'Lock up carefully and don't let anyone in. And take care!' He reached out his hand and patted her cheek. Her heart accelerated, although the pat was no more than the casual, tender caress that any man might give any nice little girl.

Angelina's eyebrows went up in mild surprise. 'Oh — caro, how charming,' she murmured, smiling with the gentle indulgence of someone observing a pet dog being given a titbit.

Suzy returned to the table and looked at the food chilling and congealing there. She felt a faint revulsion and put it all back into the heated trolley.

She could settle to nothing, not reading, nor music, nor writing a letter home. She felt deserted; raw and exposed as though pieces of her had been torn off. The sensation of being alone and abandoned cut into her deeper and deeper. She wondered if this was a terrible foretaste of how things were going to be whenever Leon was not with her. How long would the hurting last? How long did it take to shake the need of love for one special man out of your heart for ever?

Later in the big bed, under the doleful eye of the massive dark furniture, she was restless and agitated. When she finally slept, her dreams were filled with his voice as though there were to be no escape.

She overslept and woke unrefreshed.

Leon was already at the piano. Suzy felt a sharp anger towards him because she loved him and he had rejected her; for that was how she saw it. Her mind was too filled with images of Angelina to allow her to conceive of any other interpretation of his behaviour. Angelina arrived at ten o'clock and Suzy learned that Leon and she planned to spend the day together working on the Double Concerto.

'Suzy, why don't you take the day off — take a look at the city — take the car if you like.' His tone was kind. There seemed to be a lot of taking she could do.

'Thank you,' she said, refraining from adding bitterly that she could certainly take a hint and keep well out of the way.

'Suzy,' he put a restraining hand on her shoulder, but before he could speak Angelina called to him, her low, mellow voice urging him to join her at the piano without delay. He sighed and ran the hand through his hair.

Suzy felt a spark of anxiety for him. He was driving himself to the limit. He was drained and exhausted. She wished that she could help him. His eyes burned down into hers but they were full of music and tension. She felt that he did not see her at all.

'Leon! We must begin.' Angelina set the piano throbbing with an imperious, trill of summons. Leon turned in response, his face cool and determined. In a few minutes the apartment rang once again with the joy and energy of Mozart.

Suzy prepared to go out. She had no intention of using Leon's car. She would do just as she pleased, take this city by the throat if she felt like it.

But in the end all she felt like doing was sitting in miserable solitude in a street cafe drinking interminable *café-crèmes*. She dragged herself around the shops and considered queueing to take a coach to the Spanish Riding School in the Hofburg Palace where the famous

Lipizzaner stallions were kept. But the coaches seemed to be booked up for weeks ahead. There were queues too to hire a horse-drawn carriage for the customary lightning tour of Vienna. She returned to the café. At least there was a waiter there with a friendly face who looked after her well.

★　★　★

When she got back to the hotel she could hear the murmur of Angelina's low, pretty voice as she walked down the corridor outside Leon's suite. She was reminded of the warmth that was steadily growing between these two talented people.

She went straight to her room. Suddenly Leon was there with her. His hand was laid on her shoulder — just for a second. She froze into stillness.

'Had a good day?' he asked lightly.

She was silent.

'Suzy?' he murmured in appeal, wanting to be friendly, wanting her to share her day with him Why did he do this, switch her on and off like a light bulb. It was all right for him. He was simply casually friendly; he was having a wonderful time fulfilling himself in his work — and falling in love with somebody else. He had no need of her. But he was squeezing the very life from her.

'Will Angelina be staying for supper?' she asked in a voice of cardboard. 'Shall I order something to be brought up here for you?'

'Suzy! Stop it!' He touched her bare forearm with exquisite delicacy. Little licking quivers of desire shot up the limb into her chest.

Now she did turn to look at him. 'What time would you like to eat?' she repeated. She could feel the cold fire shining from her eyes, covering the brilliant flames she was determined that he should never see.

'Suzy — please!' He closed his eyes momentarily.

His voice was flat and resigned. He

looked completely exhausted. Suzy looked up at his strong six-foot frame and saw the vulnerability, the need for care and solace underneath the tough, languid, sardonic shell. Oh Leon, she thought. Let me comfort you. Let me stroke all that tension away from your face. Let me love you with my hands and my voice — and my body.

He was moving close to her, his eyes unseeing and dreamlike. That unmistakable chord which linked them was drawing tighter.

Angelina's ripe voice broke the spell. She stood just outside the door, quietly observing. 'Ah, Suzy — it is good of you to order supper. We could go out of course, but . . . well, it is so much nicer here.' She smiled encouragingly.

Her experience in dealing with servants had taught her exactly how to get the best out of them.

Suzy was suddenly tragically certain that Leon would not be needing her to provide any comfort. Why should he when he could find blissful solace with

Angelina? She imagined him laying his dark head against her beautiful rounded breasts whilst those strong, talented fingers of hers stroked his cheeks and twined themselves in the silky dark hair.

Angelina's glance moved over Leon with solicitous assessment. '*Caro*,' she murmured to him, 'you remind me of a wonderful symphony — so many shades, so many moods, so many changes of tempo — such variety.' Her graceful hands sketched out a wide arc of appreciation through the air. 'But just now you are very, very tired. You need to rest. The mood should be very slow and very gentle.' She turned her violet eyes on Suzy.

'Perhaps you would bring some drinks,' she requested softly.

'Yes — of course.' Suzy moved obediently to the tiny unobtrusive refrigerator and began to get ice for Leon's whisky and Angelina's favourite chilled moselle.

'Playing this concerto means so much to you, *caro*,' Suzy heard her tell him as they sat together. 'You are pushing yourself so hard, wearing yourself out.'

How well she understands him, Suzy thought with a mixture of admiration and gloom. Angelina was still talking as Suzy took in the drinks, but now the topic had changed. She spoke quite openly, apparently oblivious to Suzy's presence. 'This has never happened to me before you know. It is so very special.'

Suzy felt her heart spin down into a vortex of blackness. She saw grey misery stretching ahead of her — endlessly, on and on.

'But it is so fragile,' Angelina continued, 'it must be left to grow and flower undisturbed . . . '

Suzy sat in her room trying to shake that voice of whipped cream out of her head. Later, as had happened the evening before, she ordered dinner and set it out on the table as attractively as she could.

'Ah,' she heard Angelina remark

sweetly as she and Leon sat down to eat, 'This will help you to relax, Leon, then after the concert — *mio diletto* — you can start to live fully again.'

Suzy understood exactly what she was getting at. Once Leon had proved to himself that he could reach the highest level of achievement, through his performance of the Mozart — then he would be able to give in to his need for love. Love with this beautiful woman who had such depth and energy and talent — who would understand perfectly how he needed to be treated.

She poured the wine and began to withdraw.

Leon had been watching — still and silent. 'You've only set two places, Suzy,' he said softly.

'Yes, of course.' She stared at him with panic-stricken eyes and escaped without delay to sit on her bed, her feelings like a tight lumpy knot inside her.

He pursued her quietly. 'Did you have a meal out?' he asked with sharp concern.

She shook her head. 'I'm really not hungry.' She needed to be alone, could not bear to see him with Angelina for one more minute. Her eyes were full of silent entreaty as she looked up at him. 'I'd prefer to stay here and read. I'll clear all the things away later,' she added hastily, recalling that she still had jobs to do.

'Oh, little one,' he said, his eyes digging into her thoughts, his voice low and soft, 'You're very tired. Are you still ill; should I have left you in Schlezbruck?'

Suzy swallowed. 'No, I'm all right,' she stated mechanically.

'No. I don't think so.' He laid a gentle hand on her arm. The skin felt as though it were on fire under his touch. When he approached her in this tender, caring way she became unnerved, terrified that she would shatter into emotional pieces.

'Angelina's waiting for you,' she said stonily, her voice deeply rejecting under the crushing weight of her wretchedness. The last thing she wanted to do was to push him away. The last thing she wanted to offer him was coldness yet, precluded as she was from giving him the true heat of her love and desire, it seemed to be her only means of self-defence. Warm, detached amiability was no longer a viable option. 'I'll be fine in the morning,' she persisted stubbornly in distant tones.

He did not fail to catch the note of rebuff, his face settling into a mask of frozen disdain. 'Yes, I dare say you will,' he agreed. 'Sometimes, Suzy, I think you're the toughest little nut I've ever come across.' He turned roughly away from her and went to join Angelina.

Suzy sat in her room and for the first time in her life wished some of that life away — prayed for the next few days to pass quickly so that she could return to her family and give the wounds, which Leon's presence was constantly deepening, chance to close over and heal.

6

It was the day of the concert. Leon's hotel suite was alive with suspense and anticipation. Toni and Bruno arrived in the middle of the morning.

'Leon's gone out for a walk,' Suzy explained. 'He said he needed some exercise, but he'll soon be back.'

'Great!' Bruno threw himself onto the sofa, happily accepting Suzy's offer of coffee and pulling a giggling Toni onto his knee.

Suzy, dispensing coffee and slices of chocolate *torte*, wondered if these two friends of Leon would moderate their enthusiastic kissing and fondling when he returned. The two of them were currently blended together on the sofa resembling some gently panting octopus.

'I guess Leon's been real jumpy these last few days,' was Toni's opinion as she filled her wide, pink mouth with chocolate and cream. 'Just imagine playing the piano in front of all those people.'

'Yeah,' Bruno nodded, 'I've seen him strung up like a piece of wire before a big concert. Absolute hell. But the performances are always terrific. Brilliant!'

'Oh — he'll be fine,' Suzy murmured non-committally, not wishing to be drawn into any discussion about Leon. For in addition to her other feelings for him there was a fierce loyalty. And in any case, he had not been hell at all. He had been very courteous, very considerate, very distant and very much the correct employer. Suzy could find no fault with him.

But Suzy had learned in the last few days what hell was like. Hell was seeing Leon's face soften when Angelina Frascana called or telephoned. Hell was seeing how well they related to each other, how much they shared artistically, how Angelina was able to provide stimulation, reassurance and support for Leon's breakthrough into new musical territory. She saw that they were two very special people who fitted, who matched, who deserved each other.

Suzy slotted into the minor role of chief coffee provider and general dogsbody. She became skilful at taking phone-calls, deflecting casual callers and knowing when to leave Leon severely alone. She ordered tempting snacks, prepared drinks and made sure the car was topped up with petrol — ready for him to use at any time. She knew that she was doing an excellent job, but it was rather like being on the end of the chorus line in a glittering musical when all the time one wanted to be the leading lady.

'Suzy!' Toni's voice tugged Suzy's thoughts back to reality, 'I think you're even thinner than before.'

'Oh shut up,' Bruno chided affectionately, 'You've got weight watching on the brain.'

'I sure don't any more. Not since I met you.'

'I just love something to grab hold of,' Bruno chuckled.

'I've noticed,' Suzy smiled, 'It seems to happen with monotonous regularity when Toni's around!'

'Suzy,' Toni whispered urgently, 'Bruno and I are going to make it together — permanently.'

'Get married?' Suzy asked with surprise.

'I'm just thinking about it,' Bruno warned teasingly, 'Don't want to be branded as a gold digger. Makes life difficult when you fall for a girl who's loaded.'

'Oh there's no need to worry,' Toni breathed huskily, 'Daddy'll give the O.K. He always said I should choose a nice simple guy who really loves me.'

'Hey, not so much of the simple,' Bruno protested.

'Oh you know what I mean.' Toni put her hands around his face and teased his lips with her fingers. 'Mmm, you're a great big huggy bear — I could love you to bits.'

Suzy could see that Bruno was just what Toni needed; an unquestioning, loving man to cuddle up to. He would put his great paws round her and make her feel totally wanted. Leon would have been the last man she needed with his razor-sharp perception which demanded a strength and maturity Toni might never achieve in her whole life. And Toni would be so good for Bruno, cover him in adoration and provide him with the life of ease he would very much like to become accustomed to.

'You know,' Bruno said casually, 'it's time Leon got tied up. He's been free and foot-loose for too long. What do you think, Suzy?'

She shrugged, well used now to concealing the pain of loving which had become an integral part of her internal landscape.

'Yeah,' Bruno continued, 'no one should go on having such a successful time with women.' He grinned, oblivious to the fact that he was stripping

Suzy's emotions down to their bare white bones. 'It's just not fair!'

'I used to think he was a great guy,' Toni went on. 'This guy really rates, I thought. Time he got committed to one relationship — meaningful, permanent!'

Suzy permitted herself a gentle smile recalling Toni's relentless pursuit of Leon, wondering if she had had permanent commitment on her mind. No wonder he had been edgy.

'He did have a girl a year or two back,' Bruno mused, suddenly serious. 'I met her once. He seemed really keen on her. She was nice, small, ginger-haired, full of life. A bit like you, Suzy,' he laughed carelessly.

Suzy felt her pulse quicken. 'What happened to her?'

'She got killed,' Bruno said in an effort to remember. 'Car accident. I think she was driving one of Leon's cars — one of those Italian sports jobs. He was a real hell-raiser then — with cars that is. Drove like a maniac, foot hard down on the loud pedal all the time. I think he was pretty screwed up about that girl. He never mentioned her. And there were no more sports cars. Plenty of women though! One after another. Perhaps he thought that was safer.'

'That's a real sad story,' Toni said, her eyes wide with sympathy.

'Yes.' Suzy heard her own voice, very faint as though coming through a fog of confused sensations. Thoughts were lurching dizzily in her head as she reviewed this unexpected revelation. She remembered what Leon had said about a girl who had killed herself behind the wheel. It had never occurred to her that the girl had been so special to him. The intensity of his dislike of being driven at speed by a woman was now fully explained, as was something else, the reason why she, Suzy, had interested him once, just a little. She had been merely a pale image to him, a frail reflection of a tragic dead lover he had cherished long ago. That interest, that warm desire he had shown for her now seemed to dissolve into complete unreality, was crushed and swept away like the soft lumpy remnants of a child's sand castle in the on-coming tide. She had clung to those memories for consolation in the last few days and now they too were brutally stripped from her. She saw clearly now that she had never meant anything to him. Nothing at all ever.

Stunned with this fresh misery she moved like a sleep walker as the phone began to ring. She picked up the receiver and spoke correctly into it.

'Suzy, how are you?' The warm, mellow voice was unmistakable.

'I'm fine, Angelina — and you?'

'Oh yes. In fact much better than fine. I feel wonderful. May I speak with Leon please?'

'I'm sorry, he's out. He'll be back soon.'

'Oh. I see. I wonder, would you give him a message?'

'Yes.'

'Tell him that the obstacles have all

been removed and we can go ahead with the celebration tonight after the concert. He will understand.'

'Yes.' Suzy's voice trembled a little. She stiffened with self-protection. Could there be further worse hurting in store for her? This must surely be the very depths of despair that she had reached. Angelina's message seemed perfectly clear; her future with Leon must now be beautifully assured. She went to her room and sat in unthinking, trembling silence until she was jerked into alertness by the sound of Leon's footsteps in the hall, heard his dark velvety voice welcoming Bruno and Toni.

She splashed cold water on her face and brushed her hair. She was surprised to hear the piano, surprised because it was not Mozart's music, which was all she had heard recently, but something modern. The tune was arresting with a certain wistful, meditative quality about it. The singing tones of a clarinet completed the mood of gentle reflectiveness.

There was a tap on her door. Leon stood behind it. He smiled, but Suzy could tell that beneath that composed façade he was taut with anxiety. Her heart was filled with tender concern for him as she thought of the forthcoming performance and the undoubted terrors it must hold for him. If only she could hold him in her arms and kiss away the fears.

'Come and listen to this,' he told her, taking her hand and pulling her towards the drawing-room.

Bruno stood by the piano, his clarinet in his hands and his face flushed with emotion. He put the instrument to his lips as Leon sat at the piano and played from the handwritten score on the music rest. Suzy noticed the faint tremble of his fingers on the clarinet's shiny keys.

'Bruno's offering. The fruits of his labours at the villa,' Leon commented as he played the last tender chords. 'A complete re-write of 'A Little Lovely

Loving'. What do you think, Suzy?'

She shook her head in amazed admiration. 'It's just superb!' she said sincerely.

Bruno, his heart well and truly on his sleeve, gazed with trepidation at Leon who smiled sardonically and said, 'I'm inclined to agree.'

'Phew!' Bruno slumped over the piano in relief.

'You seem to have been something of an inspiration Toni,' Leon commented lightly, his tone characteristically mocking yet serious beneath the banter.

Unhampered by any doubts as to having acted as an inspiration, Toni simpered a little and smiled adoringly at Bruno.

'Naturally we shall have to await the publisher's comments,' Leon observed, 'but I think a glass of champagne would be quite in order in anticipation!'

'Terrific,' Bruno grinned, 'any excuse!'

'Shall I get it now?' Suzy asked, practical as ever.

'Oh — I think Bruno and Toni will manage,' Leon suggested. 'You look a bit whacked, Suzy.'

'Sure. Poor Suzy, you just sit tight. We'll do everything.' Toni grabbed Bruno and hauled him off in search of champagne.

'Hmm, she certainly is somebody,' Leon grinned, observing Toni's departure, the curvy bottom straining against the skin-tight denim. 'But perhaps not a body of knowledge,' he added softly, his eyes alight with mischief.

A gleam of amusement flickered in Suzy's mind but was almost instantly overlaid by the impulse to break down and weep because she loved him so much, because it was so good to be with him — because he would soon be out of her life forever.

'They'll be good for each other won't they,' Leon said, sitting down next to Suzy and wrenching her heart out with a tender glance.

'Yes.'

'Yes,' he echoed. 'Two wonderful

warm people. Warm but a little shallow,' he grinned — 'like a children's paddling pool.'

Suzy could not suppress a chuckle. There was no malice in his voice.

'That's better,' he said softly. 'I haven't seen you smile much recently.'

'Oh dear. I'm sorry.'

'Have I been working you too hard; been a cruel task-master?' he probed with gentle humour.

'No — no.' She turned away from him, sure that he would see the love springing from her eyes and desperate to conceal it. She remembered the phone call, gave him the message keeping her voice detached and clinical.

He stared at her, then broke into the warmest, softest of smiles. 'There's going to be a really special party tonight,' he said mysteriously, 'Quite a few things to celebrate.'

She held herself in rigid control. 'Do you want me to prepare anything,' she asked with cool correctness.

'No,' he said mildly, 'I just want you

to come along and enjoy yourself. We'll be able to relax then.'

This was going to be his night of triumph, Suzy thought. He wants everyone to share — even the little rabbit who caught his interest for a brief time because she reminded him of another lover.

Bruno and Toni were returning in a clatter of laughter and clinking glasses.

Suzy joined in the general atmosphere of well being and celebration for a moment then excused herself and fled quietly from the hotel. Leon had always insisted that she have some time to herself in the middle of the day, and as she had done for the last few days, she sought solace in the heart of the city.

She wandered disconsolately through the streets. Vienna was not a city to explore alone. One wanted a companion to laugh with on the breathtakingly swift trams, a drinking partner to while away the hours within the dimly lit wine bars and snug little coffee shops, a friend who knew what was what in the enticing restaurant kitchens.

She wanted Leon, of course. In the throbbing heart of the city she was gripped with loneliness and longing. Eventually she found herself making her way to her favourite little street cafe where she sat down and ordered a beer. As she sipped and reflected there was a gentle tap on her shoulder. She was startled, turned swiftly. The tall elegant man looking down at her was vaguely familiar. She frowned, trying to remember where she had seen him.

'I think we met in Hamburg,' he explained helpfully. 'My son wished to escort you one evening.' He smiled knowingly.

'Ah — I remember now,' she said, her mind running back to the meeting in the hotel foyer with the young Dutchman.

'May I get you another drink?' His courtesy was impeccable.

She smiled and nodded.

He brought two beers and sat down opposite her. 'So,' he remarked thoughtfully, 'you are the young lady who was accompanying Leon Ferrar.'

'Yes, I'm his assistant.' She was keen to disabuse him of any idea of another kind of relationship.

'Ah — I see.'

'He's playing tonight with Angelina Frascana,' Suzy told him, a bright glimmer of pride spiking inside her. 'The Mozart Double Concerto.'

'Yes, I know. My wife and I are going.'

'Oh — good. It's a very important night for him — playing Mozart.' Suzy found it a great relief to talk to a stranger about Leon. The obvious interest of her companion encouraged her to become more expansive. 'You see he's developing his classical repertoire at the moment. He's just brought out an album for young listeners. It's very good!'

Suzy was rather shocked to hear the possessive admiration in her tone. She must stop it immediately.

But the big Dutchman merely smiled approvingly. 'I'd like to get that,' he said, ' . . . when it's available.'

Suzy felt a rush of enthusiasm. 'I've got a copy,' she said, 'a first pressing.'

The man's eyes sharpened with intent interest. 'Really.'

'Signed as well,' she continued innocently.

Now the man sat up. A look of shrewd calculation came into his eyes. 'I thought he never gave autographs.'

'No — that's right.'

'You're a lucky girl.'

'Yes.' Suzy experienced a vague disquiet.

'You realise,' the man said slowly, 'that you have something very valuable there.'

'Well — yes.'

'In financial terms I mean. I'm prepared to give you a lot of money for it.'

She did not understand at first.

He named a figure.

She could not believe it. 'But why?'

'Because I can sell it for even more. Make a nice profit. I run a business in Amsterdam — jewellery, books,' he drummed his fingers in calculation on the table, 'all kinds of interesting things. I could sell that record of yours ten times over tomorrow. Especially if this concert is a success.' He watched her with the easy cunning of an experienced trader. 'I'll give you cash, English notes,' he urged, 'you can have them within the hour if you like.'

'Oh I don't know. I don't think so. No!' She jumped up and moved away from him. She was seized with indecision. How could she sell Leon's precious gift? It was all she would have left of him in the future. But the offer of the money was so tempting. It would easily pay off Graham's ever-mounting debts with a little to spare. She could buy her parents something very special. She thought of her home — her family. That was where her future lay, not with this wonderful, sexual, unconventional man who had cast a spell over her with his languid dreamy eyes, his magnetic personality and his powerful body. What would he be to her years from now — and what was she to him? Nothing.

She threw her shoulders back, rebellious and defiant.

The man sat at the table quietly waiting. 'Well?'

'Yes. Yes, all right.' Instantly she regretted the decision. But it was too late to retract. Already the man was working through the practicalities which would seal the bargain.

'Can you bring the record to the concert tonight. Meet me and my wife in the cocktail bar ten minutes before it begins?'

Suzy passed a hand over her forehead. The plans were simple and straightforward yet they seemed almost criminal. 'Yes — yes I suppose so.'

'Good! We have a deal.' He extended a heavy well fleshed hand and shook hers. 'Good afternoon.' Before she could change her mind he had strode away.

Suzy was trembling. She felt like a traitor. She had made a wonderful yet terrible bargain.

At the apartment she greeted Bruno

and Toni with almost unseeing eyes.

Toni crept into her room a little later. 'It's gonna be a great party tonight, lots of things to celebrate,' she breathed, her eyes shining blissfully. 'Leon says you're coming too.'

'Yes,' Suzy tried to appear enthusiastic.

'Will you wear the black dress, Suzy — please?'

Suzy had almost forgotten the strappy glamour gown Toni had given her. 'O.K,' she said submissively. She could not care less what she wore. Leon had arranged that she should drive him to the Concert Hall at six o'clock, then return for the others. It was already five-thirty.

She had been out for much longer than she intended. She would have to move quickly.

The black dress was rather startling. The mesh of fine straps across the front plunged into a V-shape down to the waist. Enough of the curve of her breasts was revealed to be deliciously provocative yet the dress had an elegance about it which saved it from cheap sensationalism. Although not at all Suzy's taste, she had to admit when looking in the mirror that it suited her very well — brought out the more positive and assertive aspects of her personality. In it she felt brave and purposeful and very much her own person. She fluffed out her newly washed hair and made no attempt to restrain it, let it fall in an abandoned russet curtain. Her hand rested on the stopper of the Jungle Gardenia perfume. Far too sexy and flamboyant she thought. She was past caring. Sprayed it on liberally.

The apartment seemed quiet and deserted. The family were still dressing.

Leon was sitting at the piano, staring unseeingly ahead, his body still and rigid like a piece of stone. He was dressed in a formal lightweight black evening suit, white shirt, black tie, gleaming black shoes.

Suzy felt as though her heart were in her throat as she looked at him. She could hardly speak.

'Are you ready?' she said softly, 'It's time to go.'

'Yes.' He did not turn round. He spread out his hands and contemplated their slender strength.

She wanted to put her fingers on his shoulders and massage away the taut anxiety, trace a gentle path of kisses across the skin of his neck underneath the black curls. And what is stopping me, she thought. Petty convention, natural female reticence? It was neither of those. It was the image of Angelina Frascana and the sure knowledge that Leon wanted only her.

'Are you ready?' she repeated more urgently.

He rose. He looked at her, took in the dramatic, unfamiliar image. His face darkened. Then suddenly he grinned. 'Are you sure *you* are ready, Suzy?' he asked teasingly. 'You are dressed, aren't you?' He hooked a finger casually into one of the revealing straps and gave it a playful tweak.

Suzy burned with angry humiliation. If the dress was truly indecent he should tell her. He would tell Angelina, she was sure — would care enough not to let her go out and make a spectacle of herself. She wished he would be angry, storm about and order her to change into something more modest, like a possessive lover. 'Is there something wrong with the dress?' she demanded, bitter — yet strangely hopeful of at least some opinion.

'No no — it's fine.' He spoke with disinterested impatience.

In the car he was silent and abstracted.

'Are you nervous?' she asked hesitantly after a long silence.

'Yes. But I'll be O.K.' he said in a flat voice.

'Of course you will,' she murmured.

'Suzy,' he said urgently, 'after the concert — there's a lot I want to say to you.'

She nodded. She could well imagine.

'You will be at the party, won't you. Won't hide in your room?'

'Yes,' she sighed, 'I'll be there.'

They were drawing up at the performer's entrance. A little knot of curious concert enthusiasts waited outside the unobtrusive grey door and watched the big car approach with interest. Suzy switched off the engine. She felt the crackle of tension in the silence. She turned to him impulsively. 'I won't say good luck. You've done too much good solid preparation to need luck. I hope the performance gives you all the fulfilment you could wish for.' Suzy was amazed at this little speech of hers. She realised that she was saying good-bye to him, truly wishing him happiness not just for this evening but for a whole future.

He turned his head slowly, fastened his dark eyes on her. She could see their tawny flecks in the shafts of sunshine which fell in dappled golden discs on the upholstery like a shower of coins. He leaned towards her, his intention unmistakable. Suzy was transfixed, fascinated — filled with a sense of the inevitable.

'Perhaps I don't need luck,' he murmured, 'just a little extra strength.'

His lips closed over hers as though they belonged to him.

He kissed her with all the thoroughness and dedication which he had put into his practising. When he had finished she felt that he had sucked all the strength from her. As he left the car she was trembling, her hands quivering uncontrollably on the wheel, her right leg jerking and powerless as she tried to press the accelerator.

The small crowd of onlookers gave a thin ripple of applause. Was it in anticipation of Leon's performance — or in amused approval of the one he had just given? And in the morning they would look in the newspaper and see pictures of Leon and his new fiancée and smile indulgently because they had seen him the night before toying with his attractive assistant.

How could he do this to her she

thought with desperate outrage as she guided her car through the jumble of Vienna's evening traffic. She could still feel the touch of his lips, the taste of his tongue. It was as though he had printed himself upon her so that she could never escape from him. She glanced in the rear-view mirror, passed a hand over the rounded flesh of her lips.

She felt that the signs of him would be visible there. That everyone would know how easily available he thought he was. Toni and Bruno waited on the steps, Bruno's large frame restrained for once inside a correct navy suit, Toni brilliant as a peacock in electric blue and yellow.

Suzy ran towards the lift which would take her up to the suite. 'I'll be back in a minute,' she called.

She delved in her case. Her hands were weak and wayward. She pulled out the record, glad that it was in its brown packing and that she would not have to look at the sleeve and meet the cool gaze of the man's face pictured on it.

She slipped it between the folds of her light cotton evening shawl and hoped that it would not be visible to the casual observer.

After dropping Bruno and Toni off at the concert hall's impressive main door with its softly carpeted foyer, she parked the car in the space specially reserved for it at the back of the hall, then hurried through to the cocktail bar.

The big Dutchman was already there with his wife. They smiled encouragingly.

'Ah — so you did not change your mind.' The man's manner was easy and relaxed. He was merely clinching a rather interesting and unusual deal. It meant comparatively little to him she guessed. He handed her a thick brown envelope.

Suzy licked her dry lips. She gazed about furtively — like a fox fleeing from hounds. But she saw no-one she knew. And in any case no-one was taking the slightest notice. They were all laughing and drinking. She stared at the big man.

'You must count it,' he said smiling. 'That is the usual procedure.'

'Oh — oh I see.' She felt wretched and awkward. Glancing inside the envelope she could see a number of fifty-pound notes — the correct number. It had never occurred to her not to trust the man. Her only concern had been her own treachery. She handed over her side of the bargain. She could not bear to stay any longer. 'I must go,' she muttered. She stuffed the notes in her bag and almost ran from the bar.

The concert began with a Mendelssohn overture; next was a Haydn symphony followed by a short interval. The concerto came on its own right at the end. Suzy let the first two pieces wash over her in soft waves. She sat alone and immobile during the interval, a terrible concern and anxiety for Leon gradually growing within her.

* * *

The orchestra re-assembled. After a pause the conductor appeared. He brought Angelina and Leon with him, leading each by the hand in the unselfconsciously affectionate style of musicians all over the world. A great thunder of applause broke out. Suzy sensed the emotional charge of the occasion. The audience were loving it all — the début of this lethally attractive popular music star in a truly formal classical setting in partnership with one of the best-loved and most experienced interpreters of Mozart's piano music.

Two massive shining concert-grand pianos flanked the rostrum.

The conductor invited the pianists to take their places. Angelina arranged the scarlet ruffles of her flamenco-style gown over the small leather stool, flexed her long wrists and threw Leon a gentle smile of encouragement.

A hush fell. The orchestra started on the opening passage, a rich and inviting aperitif from the string section promising even better things to come. The two soloists sat calm and expectant.

Suddenly Suzy could bear it no longer. Her treachery rose up in her throat and almost choked her. She stumbled from her seat, pushing her way towards the central gangway, tripping over elegantly shod feet, lurching against silk-clad thighs. People put their hands out in alarm and concern but she brushed them away. Her heart thrashed against her ribs. The red carpeted foyer was now almost deserted. She pulled herself together so as not to attract the attention of the stern-looking white-gloved commission-aires quietly patrolling the area.

Without any real hope of success she tried to find the Dutch couple. She went into the bar, into the cloakrooms, up and down all the corridors and staircases. Naturally it was useless. The couple, like everyone else, would be in the auditorium enthralled with the performance which was taking place. If only she could have the chance for one brief word with them — the opportunity to persuade them to take back the now detested brown envelope and return the much-cherished record into her safe-keeping. She knew in her heart that there was no chance at all of getting it back.

She waited miserably until the end of the performance. The audience spilled out of the auditorium smiling and exclaiming in delight. She scanned the throng anxiously. But there were so many exit points. It was not possible to cover them all. The mission was hopeless. Eventually, after what seemed an eternity, Bruno appeared, slightly breathless. 'I've just fought my way out of Leon's dressing-room. It looks like a florist's shop. He wants us to take a taxi home. Apparently the car is under siege. He says he'll come along as soon as he can.'

In the taxi Toni bubbled with excitement. 'I just can't believe it. He was just fabulous. And Angelina — what a fantastic figure, super dress!'

At the apartment Bruno started popping champagne corks.

Suzy had no real idea of what the plans were for the rest of the evening and she had ceased to care. She was exhausted and confused. She wanted to lie down somewhere on her own. She struggled to be sociable, gulped down a glass of champagne and found that it did little to help.

'I wish he'd hurry up,' Toni said, 'I'm starving!'

'He's probably the world's most wanted man by now,' Bruno joked. 'We'll be lucky to get any supper at all.'

'Is Angelina coming?' Toni asked curiously, 'I'd sure like to meet her.'

'Oh yes. There's a very special surprise celebration lined up so Leon told me, and she's one of the star attractions.' Bruno winked at Toni and twined his arms round her like some great loving python. 'Don't worry, girls,' he assured them. 'You'll be getting a superb dinner all in good time. I've reserved a table at the best restaurant in town. There'll be no problem, we'll be guests of the month. They'll wait for us.'

'Oh great,' Toni giggled, 'I'll go freshen up.' She departed with Bruno's eyes following her hungrily.

At last Leon arrived.

Toni and Bruno flew to greet him, almost bowling him over with hugs and kisses and thumps of congratulation.

But where, Suzy wondered, was Angelina?

Leon was carrying an armful of roses; deep, romantic-red roses. He laid them on the table then glanced across to Suzy, his eyes warm and questioning. It was a glance of intense and powerful intimacy, as though he were calling to her in spirit across the noisy enthusiasm of his friends. Her heart leapt painfully. She smiled at him. There was too much going on to do anything else.

'I do wish Angelina would come,' Toni mourned, 'I'm dying of hunger.'

'Oh, she won't be long,' Leon said, a soft, stroking calm in his voice.

'Hey, Leon. Play something for us while we're waiting. You were just fantastic tonight. I wanna go on hearing you play,' Toni appealed to him.

'Mmm,' Leon gave her a mocking stare, 'times have changed, Toni. You never used to like me to play before. Not on the piano anyway!'

'Oh, Leon!'

He laughed. 'No I'm not playing again tonight. I'm knocked out. Couldn't play another note.'

'Oh.' Toni looked truly disappointed.

'Hey — I know,' Bruno suggested helpfully, 'we could listen to your new album, Leon.'

His words struck into Suzy's consciousness like a flaming sword.

Leon smiled. He was so relaxed now, his languid assurance completely restored. 'Yes, that's a good idea. I've only got the one copy so far — Suzy has it.' He looked across at her expectantly. 'May I borrow it back temporarily?' He grinned happily, fully trusting and unsuspecting.

'Oh Suzy, go and get it,' Toni pleaded with wide eyes.

Suzy gazed at her like a rabbit mesmerised by a ferret. She realised what it meant to wish that the ground would open up and swallow one. She felt her head and shoulders droop. 'I haven't got it any more,' she said, preferring the truth as usual even in these circumstances.

There was a short, uncomprehending silence, then the buzz of talk and laughter continued.

Suzy flew to her room and sat on the bed in black despair.

Leon followed. He did not knock. He carried one of the sheaths of roses and laid it on her lap.

'No,' she whispered, 'I can't take them.'

'Suzy, what's happened? You can tell me.' He sat on the bed and regarded her with quiet concern.

She passed a trembling hand over her forehead. She found it so hard to cope when he was being tender.

'Suzy — what *is* it?' He shook her shoulder gently, as though waking someone from sleep.

'The record.' She forced herself to meet his eyes.

'Mmm?' He was smiling, sympathetic and ready to offer consolation. He shrugged. 'Listen,' he told her gently, 'if it's got damaged, don't worry, there'll be plenty more copies available soon.' His tone was kindly but dismissive. He seemed to have other things on his mind.

She realised there was still time to cover things up — but she could not bear to conceal the truth from him.

'I sold it,' she whispered.

He frowned incredulously. She waited for the anger to thunder across his handsome features. But a look of deep hurt appeared there instead.

She elaborated. 'I sold it for a lot of money because it was personally autographed.'

His wounded gaze seemed to span an eternity. He said quietly, 'I'd have given you the money if you needed it so badly — you know that.'

The crushing disappointment in his voice made her want to cry out.

'Yes,' she agreed, 'you would.' She sensed that a great chasm was opening up between them as though they were standing on separate ice-flows being moved inexorably apart by a merciless current of icy water.

They sat in motionless silence. He gave a shuddering sigh.

The doorbell rang.

'Angelina!' he said softly.

The familiar laugh rang through the apartment — warm and pretty.

Suzy gazed at him in anguish. 'I'm not coming Leon . . . I can't.'

His face began to stiffen. His eyes flashed. 'No,' he hissed grimly, cold anger breaking forth. 'I can see that. You've simply ruined everything haven't you, Suzy?'

'Yes,' she admitted tragically.

He stood still; silent and grim for a few moments. 'I'm not going to argue.

Not now,' he said significantly, flicking a glance towards the door, beyond which they could hear the never-ceasing flow of laughing chatter. 'But we've got a lot to talk about when I get back.'

He flung the roses down on the bed and strode out of the room.

Shaken and trembling Suzy listened to the sounds of gaiety echoing through the suite. The piano tinkled. Corks continued to pop. Then everything went quiet. The door slammed.

At last — they had all gone.

Suzy telephoned the airport. She counted the notes in her bag and all her other money.

She telephoned the airport again.

Then she called a taxi and packed her case.

She left him a note. A totally inadequate apology and explanation.

She took the night flight from Vienna Airport and arrived three hours later in the thin grey rain of the London dawn — utterly wretched, half starving and almost penniless.

7

It was a wet September that year. Early morning mists developed into continuous grey day-long drizzle. The burnished, dying leaves hung suspended on the trees glistening with trembling gems of moisture. Birds sat wet and huddled under the roof-tops. The year had turned, was moving relentlessly towards winter.

Suzy had not yet found a teaching job although there were one or two hopeful interviews fixed for the following month. She took a temporary part-time post at a privately run nursery school, filling in for a member of staff on maternity leave. The four sessions a week brought in enough money to make her self-supporting and provided a focus and interest for the dreary empty weeks which seemed to stretch ahead into blank eternity.

Her parents had been faultlessly tactful and unquestioning about the events in Austria. They had accepted the drama of her return to England with quiet, kindly concern. She had been surprised and blissfully relieved to find them waiting for her in the reception area at the airport. Her mother had thrown welcoming arms around her. 'Oh Suzy — are you all right? Mr Ferrar telephoned us a couple of hours ago. He thought you might be here. He sounded so worried.'

Suzy had resisted both her parents' attempts to persuade her to return Leon's call and assure him that she was safe.

'One of you do it.' She had been very firm. 'I would really prefer not to speak to him.'

Graham had bounced in to see her the next morning. 'Hey, Suze — you look frightful! What's up? What's that Ferrar chap been doing to you?'

She had turned her face away from

him, feigned sleep. She could not bear to talk about it.

Graham's troublesome problems had been resolved before Suzy's arrival. Rod Slater's final account for the damage to his car had proved to be far less than he had feared. Graham had been almost able to pay off the debt with money Suzy had already given him, supplemented with earnings from his newly acquired paper round. Graham had decided to make a clean breast of the whole silly affair to his father who had been grave and stern but basically forgiving. Suzy had filed the incident away in her memory under the mountains and molehills category. She realised now that it was fairly likely that Rod Slater had deliberately made a meal out of the incident in order to frighten Graham.

She had not felt angry about it although she was bitterly aware of the irony of the events as far as she was concerned.

Her sordid traitorous deal over Leon

Ferrar's gift had been completely unnecessary.

She wondered how long it would take for the emptiness inside her to ease. How long it would be before she ceased to think of Leon in almost every waking moment? She kept the pain carefully imprisoned. There was no-one with whom she felt able to share it. In fact she began to derive satisfaction from the very ability to shoulder the grief of separation on her own, to sense that she was strong and self-sufficient. She came to accept that he was finally and irredeemably unattainable. But sometimes the longing to hear his voice, see his lazy laconic smile, rest her eyes on the hard lines of his body, touch the silky dark hair, broke through her tough defences with a dreadful violence. The despair would pounce on her unexpectedly leaving her as broken and vulnerable as his kisses had always done.

Towards the end of the month Suzy's father was given a clean bill of health and, quite unexpectedly, offered an exciting new job by a former client of his who had set up a secondary company in order to expand his horizons and now invited his old colleague to manage the original firm whilst he devoted his energy to the new one.

'It just couldn't be better,' Mr Grey commented, glowing with satisfaction. 'I get all the interesting jobs, a nice steady salary and none of the gruesome responsibilities and hassle!' He looked steadily at his excited wife and son and then at Suzy. 'We're going to celebrate,' he said firmly. 'It's time good things happened to this family.'

He took them to a new French restaurant in the High Street.

Suzy tried desperately to look happy. She felt that she was a pretty miserable, dull person to have around at present. She was determined not to spoil her family's delight. She drank rather too much Chablis and the dull fuzziness in her head the next morning gradually developed into a thudding ache. With Graham at school, her father at work and her mother helping at an all-day Bring-and-Buy Sale she had the house to herself. The day dragged out wearily.

She tried to catch up on some reading. But her concentration seemed to be so poor at present. She found it hard to settle to anything except practical tasks. Reluctantly admitting to this sorry state of affairs she went into the kitchen and started getting out flour and sugar and butter. Graham would be home in a few minutes. She would surprise him with the delicious warm smell of home-baked scones.

The rhythmical sifting of the ingredients through her fingers soothed her. She let her thoughts drift towards Leon, tried to see his face in her mind's eye. The full image was distressingly elusive. She could imagine his lips, his nose, his tawny brown eyes, the clean line of his jaw but somehow it was never possible to put all those separate elements together to capture the essence of him. Her efforts were futile, reminding her of Graham's kitten clawing excitedly at moving shadows on the wall. There was simply nothing to grasp at.

The door bell shrilled. She frowned in irritation. It was too early for Graham, and besides he had a key. She wanted to be left alone.

She did not want to chat to some kindly neighbour — curious about her circumstances, or pay the milkman or fend off a salesman wanting to arrange for the carpets to be steam cleaned.

She opened the door with still floury hands. With trembling shock she saw the image she had tried to recapture for so long standing there before her — real and sharp, living and breathing.

'You!' she gasped, sagging in shock against the wall.

'It certainly is.' The familiar laconic smile was there, the languid, relaxed posture, the dark hair falling over his forehead as he leaned lazily against the door frame. 'I thought it was time we renewed our acquaintance.'

She brushed some stray hairs from her cheeks replacing them with delicate trails of flour.

He grinned, seemingly quite at ease.

She continued to stare at him, all her limbs quivering and powerless.

'Aren't you going to invite me in, Suzy?'

She nodded, led the way into the kitchen and went to the sink to wash her hands. She dried them, began to fuss in agitation with the kettle and cups, offering him a coffee in a shaking voice. Her mind and her heart were racing in wild circles. The pleasure of seeing him again was of such intensity that it was pain. She was more than ever aware of his quiet magnetic masculinity, the easy power of his tall lean body as he leaned up against the fridge watching her. Her hands fluttered with such violent distress that the spoons tinkled in the saucers. She knew that she still wanted him — a terrible, urgent overpowering wave of desire flooded her body.

But why had he come? What possible reason was there? It must simply be a pleasant social call. His calm manner seemed to suggest only that. And what more could there be to his visit. He was probably married to Angelina by now. The brief spark of hope that had risen up died a swift, crushing death.

He was moving towards her — sure and powerful — with that familiar unmistakable sense of purpose. The shadow of his shoulders fell across her vision, black, dominant and menacing. Suddenly his arms were around her — fierce and contention defying like circles of steel. 'Are you alone?' he murmured his voice hoarse and thick.

'Yes.' Her pulse was leaping wildly.

'Good!' He bent down and pulled her close. 'Forget the coffee!'

'No, Leon — no!' She just could not bear it all again. All the rapture and then the bitter disappointment.

'Oh yes,' he said with a grim smile, 'first things first. Time to put the record straight.' His emphasis on the word 'record' was dismayingly pointed, reawakening the shame and humiliation linked with that futile tawdry incident.

He paused and smiled at her with wicked intimidation. 'Talking comes afterwards!'

She began to struggle but he gripped her tightly, one hand pinning her body to his, the other in her hair pulling her head back to expose her face and lips.

She struggled frantically. 'Leon — what are you doing?' she cried in panic.

'Behaving like a rat,' he said with grim irony, 'because that's what you really think of me isn't it, Suzy? An A1, first-class rat. So I've nothing to lose have I? If I hadn't been such a damned fool I'd have done this weeks ago in Vienna!'

She let out a small yelp, a mingling of dismay and desire, bewilderment and self-protection. Already her heart was pounding with wanting him. But she could not relax.

For a fleeting particle of a second he hesitated. 'There's no-one else is there,

Suzy. No other man?'

She shook her head. 'No,' she moaned.

His lips pressed hers, gently but with authority. Suzy stopped her futile attempts to wriggle away from him and abandoned herself to a sweet dizzy joy that pierced into her body and limbs until it seemed that she was almost alight with a living flame of brilliance which licked into every crevice of her being. As had always happened before, she wanted to give herself up to him, surrender herself totally to his hungry embrace.

Her hands were in his silky black curls, caressing the skin of his neck, travelling wildly over his face, tracing every longed for line and curve. And as his hands roamed with firm command over her small delicate body she felt as though she were being awakened from a prolonged state of torpor and numbness.

Somewhere inside her rational brain a deep stern note of warning sounded.

She fought desperately against it for a few moments. Then she fought desperately against him.

'Stop it, Leon. Don't! You mustn't! Stop, stop!' She was battering her fists on his chest, pushing him away with her knees, trying to turn her face from his fierce kisses.

He released her then he smiled, his lazy amused smile.

Suzy had the impression that he was in full command of himself — unlike her. She was horrified at this apparently calculated self-control when she herself was drowning in a swirling dark vortex of primitive need. White-hot fury spun through her clashing nerves. Her arm flew out to strike him.

He was ready for her, caught the whirling limb and held it rigid in the air for a few seconds before forcing it behind her back.

'Right,' he growled as her eyes blazed up at him, 'I thought you were a treacherous little vixen and now you think I'm a rotten, presuming, seducing snake. Isn't that so?'

'*No!*' she cried. 'I wasn't treacherous. I didn't mean it. I was foolish and impulsive, over sentimental — over reacting — because I was hurt,' she finished in a low voice of anguish.

He gazed down at her, his breath soft and warm on her cheek. 'I guessed,' he said in a soft tender voice, 'once I started to think rationally again.'

Suzy looked into his eyes and thought she read tenderness, concern, a depth of understanding. But how could she be sure? She was still so susceptible to his infinity of charm; she did not know what she should think. She certainly did not trust herself to be guided by feelings.

Bitter turmoil swept through her.

She heard Graham's key in the lock. She froze.

'Let me go, Leon — please!'

He ignored the request. 'Have you stopped hating yourself?' he asked unexpectedly.

'Yes!' She was hot with indignation.

But he was right. She had hated herself. Now anger and anxiety replaced self-loathing.

'Please, Leon — let me go!'

Graham was calling out. 'Hi. It's me. I'm back!'

Leon pushed her away. 'Damn, damn, damn. We're always interrupted at the crucial moment. But we're going on with this later,' he stated grimly. 'I'm not leaving until I'm good and ready and it's all sorted out.'

He sat down at the kitchen table and assumed a composed, detached expression as though he were at some polite tea party.

Graham crashed through into the kitchen, flung his hold-all on the floor and gaped at Leon in excitement.

'Hullo there,' Leon said lazily.

'Hullo!' Graham's eyes shone. 'Is that your car outside? It's fantastic!'

Suzy groaned inwardly with tolerant amusement for her brother's lack of social graces. Little phrases like 'how do you do', and so on were just not in his repertoire — certainly not when there was a car to talk about instead. But then Leon had not employed any such preliminaries with her a few minutes ago had he.

'Yes. Like a drive in it?' Leon dangled the keys enticingly.

Suzy swallowed hard. She did not want Graham anywhere near Leon's new car. Neither did she want to be left alone with him on any account. The smooth, scheming rat. He knew exactly how to organise things.

Graham hesitated. 'Yes . . . no . . . yes. I'd better not. No really I won't.'

'O.K.' Leon seemed unconcerned and Suzy was unaccountably filled with disappointment.

'A new car,' she said brightly, trying to put things back on a low-key conversational footing.

'Mmm. I sold the Bentley, picked up a Porsche from the factory in Stuttgart on the way back from Austria.'

'Wow!' Graham was breathlessly

impressed with this casual juggling of prestige vehicles.

But Suzy was deeply interested now. She remembered the shocking story of the girl Leon had loved who had killed herself, reflected on his ambivalence about speed. 'I didn't think you liked sports cars,' she said in a low voice, giving him a questioning look.

He looked steadily back. 'Time to lay the ghosts,' he murmured.

She wanted to probe further but Leon turned away and fell into easy car chit-chat with Graham. There was much discussion of maximum torque and compression ratios, noise damping and ride.

Her parents returned — were warmly welcoming of the visitor who seemed disinclined to leave.

Mrs Grey buzzed about happily preparing supper, revelling in the opportunity to impress a famous guest. 'We've heard such a lot about you,' she ventured a little uncertainly with a worried glance towards Suzy, at the same time serving Leon a generous slice of the cider-baked ham which she kept in the freezer to be brought out on special occasions.

'No we haven't,' Graham cut in badly. 'Suzy won't say a word about him.'

Suzy caught Leon's sharp eye piercing her. He leaned back and gave her a sly, seductive wink.

Her face flamed with angry resentment. He was still toying with her, playing a little game of cat and mouse.

He had presumed to come to her home without warning. He had offered no explanation, no apology, no courteous preliminaries of conversation — meaningless though those inevitably were.

He had dared to touch her, awaken torturing desire, revive unbearable pain. He was cold and cruel. What else could she think?

And she still wanted him. Loved him so much that to think of any other man would have been like trying to jump off Concorde and get on a bicycle.

She tried to swallow the ham, then struggled unsuccessfully with the blackberry and apple tart.

She went to the kitchen to fetch the cheese. Her father followed.

He closed the door firmly behind him and faced her with gentle challenge. 'Suzy, what's the problem? I've never seen you like this before, — sharp-edged, bitter, angry, quite churlish really!' He smiled to temper the criticism . . .

'Oh heavens. I'm sorry!' She busied herself with the unwrapping of lumps of cheese.

'Suzy,' her father persisted firmly. 'What is it?'

She stood silent and passive.

'Something to do with Leon Ferrar?'

'Yes.' There was a painful heaviness in her throat.

'Are you in love with him?'

There was a long pause. 'Yes.'

'So — what is the problem? He's

come specially to see you.'

'No. It's just a polite call. It doesn't mean anything.' She looked at him in helpless anguish.

Mr Grey shook his head thoughtfully. 'I don't think so. He looks to me like a man who could do with a bit of help.'

'What!' She almost shrieked. Leon needing help. She could not believe it.

'Suzy, I'm a man — as well as a father. We're quite fragile creatures. Especially when we're in love. I haven't forgotten what it's like you know. He looks as though he's trying to build a bridge and you're stubbornly refusing even to approach it never mind walk across.'

His words amazed her but she was prepared to give them her full consideration. She had complete trust in his judgement.

'Yes but the problem is that I think he's married to someone else,' she said slowly, 'engaged anyway.'

'You *think*. You're not absolutely sure?'

She gaped at him. 'Well — not absolutely.'

'Right then, give the poor man a chance to tell you.' Her father looked quite stern, then he gave a broad grin of encouragement.

Returning to the table Suzy handed Leon the cheeseboard and smiled at him softly. His dark features relaxed. She sensed that strong, irresistible flow of communication between them. At the end of the meal as everyone was busy clearing away Leon leaned towards her and said impassively, 'Suzy, if I asked you to come out with me for a drive — would you say yes?'

'Yes.' She stared at him longingly.

The car was sleek and bronze and eye-catching with a dramatic fin at the back.

Leon sank gracefully into it and opened the door for Suzy.

'You could drive,' he offered, sounding quite prepared to vacate the driving seat.

She declined the offer firmly.

He frowned in agreement. 'No, you're right. Better for me to have my hands busy so I'll keep them off you for a change.'

The words were jokey and grim at the same time. She could not tell what he truly meant.

He drove up onto the road which wound along the heath. He was still and silent, absorbed in his thoughts.

Suzy became more and more certain that he was trying to find the words to tell her about Angelina.

Still he was silent. She had to break into this dreadful void.

'Leon,' she began hesitantly.

'Suzy, don't say anything for a moment — just let me get myself together. I want to tell you something first.' His tones were low, urgent and uncertain.

Suzy looked at his fierce dark profile, at his features silvery-pale in the moonlight. With warm impulsiveness she reached out her hand and stroked his cheek with great tenderness.

He retained the hand and pressed it to his lips. 'Do you hate me, Suzy?' he asked huskily. 'Do you think I was just playing with you — using you for a casual thrill?'

'I didn't know,' she whispered, 'I always felt that there was something more, something precious and special but I daren't believe it.' She stopped. He had asked another question also which required an answer. 'And I don't hate you, Leon. I love you.' She suddenly wanted him to know — even if it meant very little to him. The words were exquisitely simple. They gave her a feeling of great release.

He turned sharply towards her then pulled the car into a deserted parking spot and switched off the snarl of the engine.

She waited in desperate hope for his echo of the wonderful words she had just spoken.

He reached over gently and put his hands around her face. 'I don't know what to say,' he told her instead.

247

Through her crushing despair Suzy steeled herself for finally knowing the very worst. She would get it over right now.

'Are you and Angelina married yet?'

'What!' He looked at her incredulously, then burst out laughing. '*No!* — we were never going to be married. In fact,' he grinned wickedly, 'if we were married she'd be a bigamist!'

'What?' It was her turn to look incredulous.

'Angelina is married to Count Luigi Boscolo — a very rich Italian aristocrat.'

Suzy could not take it in. 'But — the engagement party — the night of the concert?'

He smiled. 'Yes,' he explained patiently, 'Angelina and the Count got engaged that night. His divorce had finally come through. She had been very worried about it as it had been prolonged and especially unpleasant.'

Suzy listened wide-eyed. The bleak, dark pictures in her mind began to edge aside in deference to flickers of bright new hope.

Leon was still talking. 'The divorce came through on the day of the concert — a double celebration was called for;' he ran a finger lightly under her chin, 'A triumphant performance and a forthcoming wedding.'

Suzy recalled Angelina's quiet rapture over the telephone on the morning of that fateful day. She realised how distorted and inflexible her own thinking had been.

'I thought she loved you,' she told him, 'that you loved her.'

Leon smiled tenderly. 'In a way that was true. Music — and especially making music forms strong bonds. I was very grateful for her faith in my ability. And in turn she was grateful to me. She took me into her confidence about the divorce proceedings and was glad to have a sympathetic but detached male ear. But I was never in love with her. You knew that, Suzy.'

'No, I didn't. It didn't seem like that

at all. She called you '*diletto*',' Suzy persisted stubbornly, 'It means beloved. I looked it up in the dictionary!'

'Oh darling, it didn't mean anything. Angelina is exuberant, expansive, extrovert. Her conversational style is the same. The endearments flow freely, just like her Mozart cadenzas.'

'You seemed so relaxed when you were with her.' Suzy needed explanations.

He frowned in thought. 'Yes, you're right. You see when I first met her I was so up-tight about the concerto and that damned injury. I thought I was over-reaching myself, heading for a disaster. She gave me the reassurance and confidence to carry on. But it was as one professional to another, warm teamwork — not love.' He took Suzy's fingers in his and kissed them softly. 'Oh, Suzy, it must have been hell for you too. But I was in love with you, you darling stubborn, fierce girl — all the time!'

He slid his body with swift deftness

over the gear lever and gathered her up against him. His kisses were delicious, sweet and delicate.

'Wasn't it obvious?'

Suzy remembered the passionate embraces. 'I daren't believe it,' she told him. 'I thought perhaps you made love like that with lots of girls.'

He gripped her arm savagely. 'Hell!' he snapped. 'What do you think I am — some sort of Hollywood maverick jumping from one pretty body to another. The world's greatest and most mobile lover. Oh sure — that's the image the Press like to project. After all, who's interested in a quiet good-night kiss at the door and going to bed on your own?'

'I'm sorry,' she whispered. 'I never truly believed that of you.'

'I should hope not!' he growled. He ran his hands over her body with lingering tenderness, strayed lovingly across the roundness of her breasts. 'I had it all worked out,' he said. 'Once you had stopped being my very efficient assistant, always behaving so correctly, and once I had got my classical debut sewn up I was going to sweep you off your feet — into my arms and away into the everlasting sunset!' He grinned wickedly and trailed a tantalising hand over her thigh.

Suzy drew her breath in sharply. Warm curls of desire unfurled under his touch. What other man could be so tender, so wonderfully wicked, so passionate and so gentle? She rallied from her state of adoration in order to show a little conversational sparkle. 'That sounds like a line from a Silver Linings song!' she chided.

'It probably is!' He gave a glinting smile.

Suzy stopped trying to be controlled. She wound her arms around his neck, began to search the hard lines of his face with her fingers. 'I love you, I love you,' she murmured again and again. She loosened the thin silk tie and started to undo the buttons of his shirt.

'Really, Suzy,' he drawled, 'you

redheads are so spontaneous. You must take a grip on yourself!'

She ignored him. Started on a delicious journey of kisses across the smooth male skin of his chest and shoulders.

'I love you, I love you,' she sighed over and over, nibbling and nuzzling and kissing. 'And I might even forgive you for making me so miserable!'

'*You* forgive *me*!' he exclaimed. 'What do you think *I* felt like? You were constantly rejecting me, constantly tormenting me with the sight of other adoring men. You sold my precious gift which I gave to you with the deepest sentiment and then you deserted me on my night of need and triumph!'

'Oh — Leon, darling!' She gave his ear a gentle kiss.

'That's better,' he growled. 'There'll be hell to pay later when I get you to myself with a little more room to get to work on you.'

'Umm! I can't wait!'

His voice changed to one of low

entreaty and passion. 'Suzy — I want you, body and soul. For keeps. I want to have all this life and vigour and strength and honesty of yours just for myself. I want to marry you — soon, very very soon!'

She buried her head against his chest.

He pulled away after a while. 'Suzy — you're not saying yes.'

'Is there any need to say anything. Don't you know the answer Leon?'

'Oh Suzy — darling!'

'What about the other girl — the one who died in your car,' she asked softly, 'Bruno told me the story.'

He gazed deeply into her face. 'She was special. I loved her, but that's over now — and it's you that I love. Very very much!'

Suzy was driven to question him further. She needed finally to dispose of all her uncertainties about his other ladies. 'What about Toni?'

'Oh — that poor girl,' he groaned. 'I was so sorry for her. She was so alone, so hungry to be wanted. I met her at a party. She had just been ditched by some international play-boy. She looked as though she was going to pieces. It seemed as if she had arrived gift-wrapped solely for my attention and protection. Of course if I'd had any sense I'd have run a mile right then!'

'Oh Leon,' she teased, 'you weren't just a rescue society, were you? After all she was fantastically pretty with a super figure!'

'True,' he agreed, 'a dish — if not a four-course dinner. But I'd soon had more than enough. She wanted to own me, drown me in a great big scented bath of love with the warm water tap full on all the time. Most men would have given their last penny to have wallowed. But it wasn't for me. I wanted to run. Fast! And then you came along. I was so resentful about her persistent clinging on to me. I was out of my mind with fury sometimes about the sheer damn bad luck of the whole ironic set-up. I was desperate to be totally free. Free to take notice of you. Can you understand that, Suzy? I'm not a cold-hearted snake. I knew that's what you might have thought. What everyone thought perhaps.'

'No,' she murmured, 'you're not. You're wonderful.'

'You teased me dreadfully,' she complained softly.

He sighed. 'It seemed the only way I could make contact with you. After Amsterdam you were so cool, so correct. You wouldn't let me near you. All I could do was tease!'

'Yes,' she smiled, 'and all *I* could see was Angelina. I can see now how it must have been for you; one rejection after another.'

'Exactly.' He kissed her very tenderly. 'I wanted you, Suzy. I wanted you so much. I longed to take you to bed and make you happier than you could ever have dreamed of.'

Suzy gave a little moan.

'But I had to wait,' he continued. 'You would have felt cheap, you would have thought I regarded you as an easy lay — a girl of no worth.'

'Yes.' She saw no point in disagreeing.

'You were like a breath of fresh air to me after the spoiled, provocative women in my world. You made me feel like a man who could find his way again. You looked at me and saw the person underneath and all his flaws. You were honest and critical. You dared to judge me for what I was.'

'I made you angry,' she told him gently.

'Yes! Suddenly I had to take a cool look at myself. I had to be restrained and cautious. I had to teach myself to wait for something worth having. Was I wrong, Suzy?'

'No, of course not.'

They sat in silent reflection, fully at ease with each other.

'Are Toni and Bruno still together?' she enquired.

'Mmm,' he grinned, 'true love!'

Suzy was glad. 'I'm really happy for them,' she said, 'I like them both so much.'

He regarded her with devouring

tenderness. 'You're a very generous-hearted person,' he murmured stroking her cheek.

'I missed you,' she whispered, 'I missed you terribly.'

'I know the feeling,' he breathed into the warm skin of her throat.

'Why come today though. Why wait so long?'

He sighed deeply. 'Bruno came to see me today. He looked as though he had the exclusive world rights to happiness. He kept mentioning Toni's name, letting his voice caress it as though it were a song. It reminded me what torture it was without you . . . ' he stopped and drummed his fingers on the wheel.

Suzy laid her arms tenderly over his shoulders. 'Go on!'

'I wanted to come and see you every single day. But you wouldn't speak to me on the phone. You never got in touch. I lost hope. I buried myself in work.'

'Yes, don't stop!'

He smiled ruefully. 'This morning watching Bruno, I thought it was time to swallow the futile masculine pride. What is there to lose, I told myself; I'll go and take the girl by storm!'

'You certainly did that!'

'Yes but it worked, didn't it?'

'What do you mean?'

'Stopped you feeling wretched and guilty — got you feeling angry instead.'

She chuckled. 'Yes — I needed that. I hadn't realised. I felt so desperate about selling the record. Felt that I would never forgive myself. I still feel a little bit bad — even now.'

'Don't worry. There'll be plenty of time for retribution — later.' He grinned with mischievous menace.

Suzy felt a sharp quivering thrill at the silky threat in his words.

He sighed. 'I suppose I'll have to take you home soon.'

She consulted the clock on the dashboard. He was right.

And there was still so much to say. But there was a lifetime to say it in.

They did not need to rush.

A deep contentment was flowing through her body at his nearness, the wonderful individual smell of his skin and hair.

'Leon,' she murmured thickly as his tongue probed her mouth with soft warmth, 'is it true?'

'What?'

'That you're the world's greatest lover?'

'Naturally — a bit out of practice though.' His arms closed around her, hard and demanding. But his touch was one of the purest, softest desire — as gentle as a golden shaft of sunshine. His hands moved over the slopes of her hips.

'Aah, you. Just you,' she breathed.

'You won't be disappointed my darling, I can promise you that.' He pulled away from her with lingering reluctance.

Through the window she could see the stars massed in trembling points over the hushed, darkened heath. It was a world of satin darkness, enclosing and enfolding them in its embrace; a world strangely full of brilliance and warmth, unlike the bleak mornings of pale sunshine when he had been absent.

She put her hands sweetly around his face — this man, with whom there was a world to share — for ever.

THE END

We do hope that you have enjoyed reading this large print book.

Did you know that all of our titles are available for purchase?

We publish a wide range of high quality large print books including:
**Romances, Mysteries, Classics
General Fiction
Non Fiction and Westerns**

Special interest titles available in large print are:
**The Little Oxford Dictionary
Music Book, Song Book
Hymn Book, Service Book**

Also available from us courtesy of Oxford University Press:
**Young Readers' Dictionary
(large print edition)
Young Readers' Thesaurus
(large print edition)**

For further information or a free brochure, please contact us at:
**Ulverscroft Large Print Books Ltd.,
The Green, Bradgate Road, Anstey,
Leicester, LE7 7FU, England.
Tel:** (00 44) **0116 236 4325**
Fax: (00 44) **0116 234 0205**

FORBIDDEN LOVE

Zelma Falkiner

By the time Lyndal Frazer learns the identity of the stranger who rescued her and her sheepdog, Rowdy, from drowning, it is too late. She has fallen half in love with a sworn enemy of her ailing father. Torn between growing attraction and duty, Lyndal chooses family loyalty. But Hugh Trevellyn has made up his mind, too; a bitter feud will not be allowed to come between them.

A MAN TO TRUST

Angela Dracup

Alexa Lockton has a thriving car business and her fiancé, Royston Wentworth, is an eminently suitable future husband. But when she employs Rick Markland to work in her garage, her ordered world crumbles. Against Royston's cautious prudence, Rick encourages bold expansion at Lockton's. Alexa is caught between the two men — for she finds that Rick is compellingly attractive and, as she plans her forthcoming marriage, she begins to wonder how long she can resist his magnetic appeal.

THE LONELY MAN

Paul Blackden

When Harry Hobart, a teacher in a reform school, gets into trouble, he thinks that the police may be after him. He runs away to Yorkshire, buys a caravan and becomes a person 'of no fixed address' . . . In a York pub, Harry encounters Loraine, miserable and suicidal after being jilted. She sticks with him . . . Harry and Loraine are contrasting characters. She thinks he's a fuddy-duddy. He thinks she is over-sophisticated. But as they travel together, they come to admire one another, an admiration which turns into lasting love.